QUEST
FOR THE
NEPTIUS

A.H. BENJAMIN

NOTABLE KIDS PUBLISHING
PARKER, COLORADO

Quest For The Neptius ©2023 A.H. Benjamin and Notable Kids Publishing, LLC

Quest For The Neptius
Ages 8+ Young Reader
Library of Congress Control Number: 2023930309
JUVENILE FICTION / Fantasy & Magic/ Legends, Myths, Fables/General
ISBN 9781733354875

Benjamin, A.H.

Summary: A caring, curious, and brave eleven-year-old girl's summer stroll on a quiet beach becomes an epic adventure that pulls her into a mysterious undersea world. Lured by the simple sounds of a unique seashell, she finds herself pulled into a battle between an ancient marine species and advanced life forms not of this planet. Her survival and only path home is that of legends as she befriends magical creatures and battles an evil nymph while in quest of a simple flower.

Cover art by Peter Trimarco ©2023
Edited by Caitlin Berve and Peter Trimarco
Printed at Rightol, in China
Notable Kids Publishing, P.O. Box 2047, Parker, Colorado 80134
303.840.5787 www.notablekidspublishing.com

CHAPTER ONE

Marissa couldn't have missed seeing the seashell. It lay upon the wet sand as if a careful hand had placed it there on purpose, for her to see. Had it not been so beautiful and so quaint-looking, she would've perhaps asked herself, *Why isn't it buried in the sand like the other seashells? The morning tide has already been up and is now ebbing.*

But she didn't—she merely gasped when she caught sight of it.

"Wow!" she said over and over. Then, very carefully, she squatted in front of the seashell for a closer look.

Marissa turned eleven that summer, and in all her years of collecting seashells, she had never come across one remotely like it. She thought its beauty was astonishing. Slightly bigger than a golf ball, it was shaped like a snail shell, but slightly pointed at one end. It had colorful stripes wrapped round it, and speckled between these were dots of various sizes and every color imaginable. Marissa noticed the colors were iridescent—at the slightest move of her head both dots and stripes changed hues. Their brightness also changed, constantly and rhythmically. Because of this effect, the whole seashell seemed to throb and pulsate, giving the impression that it was breathing. Marissa realized something else—she could detect a hum emanating from the seashell. It appeared to vary in both tone and pitch, almost in accord with the fluctuating brightness.

For a long time, Marissa could only stare at this remarkable seashell, fascinated beyond limit. Then, tentatively, she stretched a trembling hand towards it. She half expected it to scuttle away on invisible legs. It didn't and she picked it up. For a seashell, it was surprisingly heavy. And it didn't feel like one either. The shell had a velvety texture similar to the skin of a peach. Yet, it was as hard as a stone.

"What a strange seashell," she uttered as she began to examine it, turning it this way and that.

"Pretty, aren't I?"

Marissa felt her heart leap into her mouth, and she sprang to her feet. There was such an incredulous look on her face as she stared at the seashell. Did she really hear something?

"You! You—did you speak?" she blurted out in disbelief. "No, no, of course not! What am I saying?" She looked all about, but the beach was deserted—it was still early.

Then the voice spoke again, hollow and distant, yet

so close. "I was beginning to get worried, you know. Thanks for picking me up," the voice said, sounding genuinely grateful.

Mouth-agape, Marissa stared at the seashell again, hardly believing her ears. "You mean... er... it's really you speaking?" she asked, her voice little above a whisper.

"Yes, of course," was the reply.

"But you're only a seashell!" cried Marissa. "And seashells don't talk. Of course, not...it's absurd!"

"Absurd?" repeated the seashell indignantly. "Let me tell you, young lady, that I am certainly no ordinary seashell. But never mind, this is hardly the time to discuss such a trivial matter. The important thing is you picked me up and you're going to help me."

"Help you?" frowned Marissa. "Help you do what?"

"To go back to the sea, of course," replied the seashell as if this was the most obvious answer in the world.

Marissa was getting more and more confused. "Oh," was all she could say.

"Perhaps I had better explain," began the seashell. "First of all, let me introduce myself. My name is, er...call me Periwinkle if you like. And briefly my problem is this— the Sea-Queen has banished me from the sea..."

"Why?" interrupted Marissa.

"Oh, it's not really important," replied Periwinkle in a matter-of-fact tone. "My plight at present is that I cannot go back to the sea until I have accomplished a good deed. If I don't do that, I shall be stuck here for the rest of my life, which I assure you, will be very short indeed. But I hope this won't happen. I'm relying on you to help me. Will you?"

"How?" asked Marissa, a little dismayed.

"It's quite simple really," he said. "Just let me grant you a wish."

"Is that it?" laughed Marissa, quite relieved.

"Yes, that's it! You see," explained Periwinkle, "if I grant you a wish, that will be my good deed. And thus, I will be able to go back to my world."

Marissa giggled. "You sound like the genie in the bottle! He always grants wishes to those who free him."

"Never mind him," cut in Periwinkle hastily. "Please, do hurry up—time is short. If you have a wish, let me hear it. I shall grant you it without fail."

"Well…" began Marissa. She thought for a moment or two. "Yes, I do have a wish. I wish to visit the undersea world someday. I would love to do that!"

"Perfect!" said Periwinkle, and Marissa was almost certain he sounded relieved for some reason. "We'll go right away. The sooner the better!"

"Now?" cried Marissa, surprised. "I'll have to tell my aunt first. I'm spending the summer holidays with her. I always…"

"No, no," Periwinkle told her. "No one else must know about my good deed! That's a condition set by the Sea-Queen herself. Besides," he added, "what are you going to tell your aunt? That you're going to visit the under-sea world with a seashell? A talking seashell? Ho, ho!" he chuckled. "She'll think you've gone soft in the head. You'll probably end up at the doctor's!"

"I guess you're right," smiled Marissa, imagining the look on her aunt's face. Still not sure if this little conversation was real or imagined, Marissa agreed. "OK, we'll go now."

"Splendid!" cried Periwinkle. "Don't worry, we won't be long. Now if you walk into the sea, I'll do the rest."

Marissa did as asked. "Good thing, I have my bathing suit on!"

A moment later, Marissa was wading through the water which had receded further down. It was a bit cool, but not unpleasant.

"That's far enough," said Periwinkle. "Now I would like you to be very quiet. I require total concentration!"

Marissa stood still, hardly daring to breathe. *What was Periwinkle up to*, she wondered. *Why am I listening to a seahell?*

A moment later she began to feel a tingling sensation in the hand in which she was holding the seashell. It was vibrating, she realized, and very rapidly. Marissa felt as if a mild current were running through her hand, then the sensation spread to her entire body. At the same time, Marissa could hear a hum, like the droning of a bumblebee, but much lower in tone. It was Periwinkle.

"What's he trying to do?" whispered Marissa, a little puzzled.

As for reply, there was a loud splash a few yards away, and the head of a large dolphin broke out of the water.

Marissa started, uttering a small cry of surprise. But the dolphin looked more surprised.

"Scales and fins!" he exclaimed when he caught sight of Marissa. "You're a land mortal! How did you know the call of the sea? For you did call me, didn't you?"

"Don't be a fool!" spoke Periwinkle before Marissa could reply.

She would not have been able to anyway—she was utterly flummoxed. First, a talking seashell and now a talking dolphin! *I must be dreaming!* she thought.

"It is I—Periwinkle!" answered the seashell. "The land maid is with me."

The dolphin cocked his head to one side, not quite understanding.

"Peri– who? Oh, you mean the Chosen," he said. With swift flaps of his tail, he swam closer to Marissa. Not taking his eyes off her, he addressed Periwinkle. "I see you have been successful. The Council will be…"

"Hold your tongue!" snapped Periwinkle.

"Oh, I, er, sorry," apologized the dolphin, quite red-faced.

"What is he talking about?" frowned Marissa, looking suspiciously from one to the other.

"Don't take notice of Delta," Periwinkle told her. "He just likes making things up. Some kind of a joker, he is."

Delta nodded vigorously, a broad, unconvincing smile on his face. "Oh, I love joking." he grinned at Marissa.

"Let's not linger," urged Periwinkle. "We've already

wasted enough time."

"Quite right, quite right," agreed Delta. "Climb on my back, land maid, and hold on tight. What's your name, by the way?" he asked as Marissa readied her herself to climb on the dolphin's back.

"I'm called Marissa."

"Marissa?" repeated Delta. "Mmm. I like that!"

"Thank you," said Marissa, rather absently. She was too busy making herself comfortable. She sat astride Delta with her long legs clamped tightly around his body. With her free hand, she held on to his dorsal fin. *Was that how one rode a dolphin?* she wondered. Well, she would soon find out. "I think I'm ready," she said finally, her voice quavering with nervousness. She still didn't quite believe all this was actually happening to her.

"All right, Delta," said Periwinkle. "You can go now and at full speed!"

Delta didn't wait for a second command. He spun round so briskly that Marissa nearly fell off his back. Then, with swift flaps of the tail, he skimmed torpedo-like through the water, leaving a narrow, frothy wake behind him.

Never in her life had Marissa experienced such an exciting feeling, partly because of the prospect of her dream-like adventure, and partly because of the speed at which Delta was going. Her long, dark hair flying wildly behind her, she felt like a sea-queen. She asked herself again, *Is any of this really happening? Or is it just a dream perhaps?* She didn't care which, she felt so elated.

Glancing back, she saw the beach receding rapidly. It was still deserted, apart from an old man and a dog. Soon they looked no bigger than two matchsticks. She could just spot her aunt's bungalow nestled in a shrubby hill. White-washed, it glistened dazzlingly in the early sunlight.

Marissa smiled, wondering what her aunt was doing now. *She certainly could not guess what I am doing!* she thought.

CHAPTER TWO

Delta sailed through the sea, covering a great distance in a seemingly short time. Soon all Marissa could see around her was a vast stretch of blueness. Sea and sky merging together, and Marissa could hardly tell which was which.

"Time to dive in," piped Delta, more to himself than anyone else. And so saying, he plunged through the water.

Suddenly something dreadful dawned on Marissa— she couldn't breathe underwater! Of course, she couldn't! And Delta was already several feet deep in the sea.

How stupid of me not to have thought of that, she chided herself. *Now I'm in a proper fix!*

As though reading her mind Periwinkle said, "Relax, Marissa. No need to hold your breath."

Goggle-eyed Marissa glared at him. *What else did you expect me to do?* she felt like saying. *I'm not a flipping fish!*

"You'll explode if you hold your breath any longer," said Periwinkle calmly.

"Mmmm!" went Marissa, shaking her head. Her face had turned a deep purple and her brown eyes had grown as big as saucers. "Mmmmmmmmmmmmm!" she kept on.

"Please, let go of your breath!" cried Periwinkle, quite alarmed this time. He had to be, as Marissa squeezed him so tightly he feared she was going to break him to pieces, hard as he was. "Please, do so!" he begged. "Now!"

At last Marissa did so, not because of Periwinkle's pleas, but simply because she could no longer hold her breath. Panicking, she began to cough and splutter, gulping plenty of sea water down her throat.

Soon, however, she realized she could actually breathe underwater. At first, she was a bit apprehensive, taking only short, cautious breaths—then deeper and deeper ones, until she found herself breathing just as easily as if she were on land.

Relieved and amazed, Marissa began to laugh.

"I can even laugh underwater!" she cried and laughed all the louder. "I can speak too. I can't believe this is true." She felt so excited she kissed Periwinkle.

"Please don't do that," objected the seashell, but he didn't sound as if he really minded.

"Sorry," giggled Marissa. "But please tell me how come I can breathe underwater? Surely, it's contrary to nature."

"Is it?" said Periwinkle, casually. "But you're doing so now."

"I know that," said Marissa. "But how do you explain it? I mean I'm not a fish. I need air to survive.

"You mean oxygen," corrected Periwinkle. "There's plenty of it in the water. In fact, there's more oxygen in water than in air. It's just a matter of knowing how to extract it. What do they teach at school these days?"

"You sound like my father!" retorted Marissa. "All I wanted was a simple answer."

"I'm afraid the explanation is far more complicated than you think," Periwinkle told her. "At any rate, I couldn't tell you the reason. It's a profound secret of the undersea world. Revealing it to you—or any land mortal for that matter would be most unwise. However, I can tell you this. You are able to breathe underwater only because you're holding me."

"You mean if I let go of you, I'll drown!" said Marissa, alarmed.

"If you put it that dramatically, yes," answered Periwinkle. "So, please, make sure you don't lose me—otherwise you're lost too!"

"Charming," muttered Marissa, worried. "What are you? A magic seashell?"

"Please, don't mention magic," chimed in Delta, who had been quiet all this time. "It gives me the creeps. Magic is wicked. Sooner or later, it turns people bad, just as it did with…"

"Be quiet!" snapped Periwinkle, so sharply that Delta swam all the faster to hide his discomfort. "When will you learn to keep your mouth shut?"

Her curiosity aroused, Marissa was about to say something, then thought better of it. *I just wish they weren't so secretive*, she thought, annoyed.

"Now what was that you asked me?" said Periwinkle peevishly. "Ah, yes. No, I'm not magic. Not in the sense you think, anyway. Perhaps I will be able to tell you some other time. But please not now."

"All right," agreed Marissa. "What about you, Delta, how come you can breathe underwater? You shouldn't be able to because you're a mammal and not a fish."

"That's correct," replied the dolphin. "The same as you. I can only do that temporarily. Thanks to…"

"Enough!" said Periwinkle sharply. "Please stop asking questions, land maid," he told Marissa. "The main thing is you are in the undersea world where you wished to be. So why don't you make the most of it? Enjoy yourself."

Marissa shrugged. "Oh, well, maybe he's right after all," she mused quietly. "Besides, if a seashell and a dolphin can talk, why shouldn't I be able to breathe underwater? That's more plausible."

And so, she decided not to ask any more questions—for the time being, anyway.

Instead, she began to take notice of her surroundings. She thought they must have been several fathoms beneath the sea, yet it was quite bright at this depth. The water was predominantly green, she noticed, but now and again it sparkled with a display of magnificent colors. She guessed it was due to the effect of the sunlight upon the undersea current.

For the first time, Marissa seemed to realize she could see as clearly as if she were wearing swimming goggles. Also, she was surprised the salty water did not sting her eyes. She didn't even feel wet. Strangely enough, it was as if she were gliding through space rather than water.

"Oh, well," uttered Marissa. "This still could just be a dream."

She noticed how friendly and unscared the fishes were. Playfully they came to brush against her legs and wriggle under her arms. Their skins were slightly rough, but she didn't mind that at all. It was just like being licked by a kitten, which she found a little bit ticklish. So whenever a fish came in contact with her skin she laughed.

Presently a beautiful sea-snake came to join the fun with the other fishes. It was about four feet long, with black and white stripes and yellow protruding eyes. Marissa was not really keen on snakes, but this one looked so friendly with its smiling face and funny eyes that she didn't mind when it began to slither playfully under her arms and around her waist, tickling her all the more.

Then, as she happened to look ahead of her, she spotted two sea-horses swimming in her direction. They looked quite comical, bobbing up and down almost in accord. As they came closer, she saw they were about a foot high with golden brown scales and sweet-looking faces. Their tails were curled up, almost like upside down question marks.

"What beautiful creatures," smiled Marissa, looking back to watch them swim away. She noticed the fine, delicate fins on their backs, flapping very rapidly like the wings of a hummingbird.

"Oh, no!" cried Delta all of a sudden.

"What is it?" asked Marissa, surprised.

"Look what's coming towards us," replied the dolphin.

Looking ahead, Marissa saw a dark, ominous shape approaching. It grew larger and larger as it drew closer. Frightened fish scattered clear of its path as it glided through the water with what looked like huge, powerful wings. It reminded Marissa of a giant bat.

Delta was trying desperately to avoid it. But every time the dolphin changed direction the dark shape did likewise, as if on purpose. Nearer and nearer, it came—a huge mass of dark brown flesh, steering relentlessly towards them.

Collison looked inevitable. However, at the last second Delta briskly swerved to one side, missing the creature by mere inches. As it swept past, it created such a violent whirlpool that Marissa was nearly thrown off the dolphin's back.

Shocked and bewildered, she turned round to see what it was. But the creature was already a distance away, its long, pointed tail swishing behind it.

"Stupid, clumsy creature!" muttered Delta angrily.

"What on Earth was that?" asked Marissa, shaking a little.

"Only a ray fish," answered Periwinkle, unperturbed by the incident.

"Wow, as big as that?" gasped Marissa. "It must've been at least twelve feet wide!"

"Their trouble is just as big," said Delta, seething with rage. "They're a hazard to sea traffic, always causing trouble. I can never seem to avoid them!"

"Stop moaning," rebuked Periwinkle, "and let's move on."

"All right, all right," said Delta, reluctantly.

After he had pulled himself together, they resumed their journey through the sea. Again, the fish came to play around them as if nothing had happened at all.

***

Marissa began to lose all track of time, wondering how long she had been in the undersea world. She couldn't tell—sometimes it seemed ages and sometimes just a few minutes.

Though enjoying herself, Marissa didn't want to stay too long. Her aunt would be worried about her. Perhaps she already was. Marissa was fond of her aunt and the last thing she would want was to upset her.

Just then her thoughts were distracted when she heard soft, sweet music the likes of which she had never heard before. Fascinated, she strained her ears to listen, wondering who could play such wonderful music. She soon found out. Sitting on a golden, sandy mound not far ahead was what Marissa thought was a young girl, playing the harp. Then, to her great surprise, she saw it was a mermaid! She could hardly believe her eyes.

Here, for some reason, Delta slowed down and Marissa was able to have a good look at the mermaid. She thought she was astonishingly beautiful. Her long, wavy hair was the color of molten gold and entwined in it was what looked like red and pink lily-shaped flowers. Her skin was milky white and her eyes were the color of sapphire, which sparkled like jewels. Her silvery tail was lithe, and she moved it about, making it shimmered with all the colors of the rainbow.

She was singing as she played the harp, while music and voice blended together in such a harmonious tune that Marissa could hardly distinguish one from the other. Overwhelmed and totally entranced by the melodious music, Marissa had a sudden, strong urge to jump off Delta's back and join the mermaid. She thought she could sit beside her and listen to her forever.

"Take hold of yourself," Periwinkle told her as though reading her mind. "I know you land mortals go mad for the mermaids' songs. You just can't seem to resist them. That's very dangerous!"

"It's the sweetest music I've ever heard!" confessed Marissa, thrilled beyond imagination. "It's almost magical, or perhaps it is. Anyway, I thought mermaids were only a myth, like other sea creatures."

"Sorry to say," stated Delta bluntly, "but you land mortals are ignorant. You don't really know much about our world. Moreover, you believe us to be dumb creatures. But that is not so. I can assure you, we are just as intelligent and civilized as you are. Only our ways of life and mode of behavior are different from yours. Isn't that correct, Chosen?"

"You never learn, do you!" said Periwinkle. He sounded quite exasperated.

However, Marissa didn't seem to notice how Delta had addressed the seashell.

"Perhaps," continued Delta, "when you get back to your world, you can tell your people about us."

"Are you kidding?" laughed Marissa. "They would never believe me. They would think I'm crazy or something!"

"There you are!" cried Delta triumphantly. "Exactly my point. Your people believe only in themselves. No, you'll never learn about our world with your superior attitude."

Before Marissa could reply, a group of mermaids suddenly appeared out of nowhere. There must have been a dozen of them, she guessed. They noisily swarmed around her, chattering excitedly between them. They all looked alike, with golden hair and sparkling blue eyes and bright silvery tails. Marissa could hardly tell one from the other.

"A maid from the land! A maid from the land!" they kept saying, over and over again, pointing and giggling.

They looked even more surprised than Marissa.

"Please, ladies, please!" pleaded Delta, slowing down. "Lets us pass through, we're in a hurry!'"

The mermaids took no notice of him, venturing even closer to Marissa. Out of curiosity they touched her hair and poked here and there as though to find out what she was made of. They were particularly interested in her legs, but tempted as they were, they dare not touch them.

"She has sticks instead of a tail," remarked one, pointing to Marissa's long legs.

"All land mortals have," said a second. "They use them to walk on land as we use our tails to swim."

"It must be painful," said a third, grimacing.

"I don't suppose so," corrected a fourth. "Why, our tails don't hurt when we swim, do they?"

They all burst out laughing, thinking it was funny.

Amused, Marissa laughed too.

Just then there was a high-pitched noise, like that of an old kettle that had come to the boil, but much louder. The mermaids' laughter turned into shrill cries, and they fled in all directions. In a few seconds they were all gone.

Marissa was utterly puzzled.

CHAPTER THREE

The whistling-like noise continued. It grew higher and higher in pitch, until Marissa could no longer bear it. She thought if it persisted it would burst her eardrums.

"What is that?" she yelled, a grimace wrinkling her face. "I wish it would stop!"

As if in reply, the horrible noise did stop.

"Ah, there they are," said Delta. "About time too!"

At first Marissa didn't know what he was referring to. But as she looked ahead, she spotted a dozen fish or so coming towards them—one leading and the rest following behind in pairs.

As they came closer, Marissa thought they were the strangest looking fish she had ever seen. Slightly larger than Delta, they had blue bodies and yellow heads, the latter deeply furrowed. Their eyes were black-ringed, like those of a raccoon. The oddest thing about them was that they all had some sort of beards. These were a deep crimson, about a foot long and slightly curled at the tip.

Despite their strangeness Marissa thought they looked somewhat impressive. They seemed strong, capable, and well disciplined.

Delta stopped, and the leader came to meet them. The rest remained a short distance away, still in formation and looking vigilant.

"I'm glad you came to our rescue, Officer Tarak," said Delta. "Those mermaids can be a nuisance sometimes."

Tarak didn't seem to hear him. He looked more interested in Marissa. He stared at her with his dark-ringed eyes. While doing so, he stroked his beard with a long fin. His head furrowed all the more.

Marissa felt uneasy. She wished he would stop staring at her like that.

To break the ice, she said, "How do you do? My name is Marissa. Nice to meet you!"

Tarak ignored her completely.

Then at last spoke, "The land maid... she looks young." He was obviously addressing Periwinkle, who replied, "That couldn't be helped. Please, do not delay. Escort us to the Palace."

"Yes, of course," complied Tarak, nodding. Without turning round, he waved a fin to summon the other fish.

As though they knew what to do, they split into two

single files and lined themselves on either side of Delta. Marissa couldn't help noticing one of them had a red cord around his head with a quaint-looking object attached to it. She guessed it was the device that had made that horrible noise earlier on.

"Let's go," ordered Tarak. Another wave of the fin and he led the procession away.

Marissa felt uncomfortable. Every time she glanced left or right, she noticed the strange fish staring at her—and not just out of curiosity, but with a wondering expression on their faces. She had a gnawing feeling that something was not quite right, but she couldn't put her finger on it.

Something smells fishy here, she thought, and she almost giggled at the idea.

"Who are they?" she whispered to Periwinkle, holding him closer to her mouth.

"The Royal Guards," he informed her. "They are escorting us to the Palace, Her Majesty's residence."

"Your queen lives in a palace?" Marissa couldn't hide her surprise.

"Yes, of course," replied Periwinkle indignantly. "I suppose your king or queen also lives in a palace."

"Yes, but we are..." began Marissa, then stopped. She was about to say 'civilized beings' but she remembered what Delta had said earlier and thought better of it lest she would hurt Periwinkle's feelings.

"Yes, you are..." prompted Periwinkle, still waiting for a reply.

"Er, it doesn't matter," said Marissa. After a short pause she asked, "But tell me, why do they refer to you as the Chosen?"

Periwinkle was silent for a moment as though debating where to start.

"Very well," he sighed. "I might as well tell you the truth now. I'm called so because I have been selected by the House of Lords to accomplish an important task. And that is to bring a land mortal to the undersea world."

"You mean me?" asked Marissa.

"Well, any mortal," replied Periwinkle. "But in this case, it's you. And I'm glad about that because I like you."

"Me too!" piped Delta who was listening.

"Oh, thank you both!" said Marissa sarcastically. "That's just charming!"

"Sorry for lying to you and tricking you," apologized Periwinkle. "Believe me, I had to. You see, we desperately need your help. It's a matter of life or death."

Marissa looked more and more confused. "I don't understand," was all she could say.

"I shall explain," said Periwinkle. "It's a long story so I'll have to start from the beginning. It happened a long time ago, in the times when mermaids were allowed to be seen by land mortals. Now it's forbidden by the Laws of the Sea. Mermaids used to swim to the surface of the sea and sit on rocks. When they espied ships sailing by, they would begin to sing and play the harp so beautifully and charmingly that sailors were unable to resist the melodious music. They would forsake their ships and try to join the mermaids, who would then dive deep into the sea, and the sailors would try to follow them. Sadly, when they swam too deep, the sailors drowned.

The mermaids couldn't understand why, and they would lament and sing sad songs to mourn the dead sailors. Yet, they did that again and again and as a result more sailors drowned. Of course, the mermaids didn't mean that to happen."

Here Periwinkle paused as though to get his breath back so to speak. He then went on,

"Now I come to the turning point of the story. There was this young and beautiful mermaid whose father was a powerful lord who knew every secret of the sea. He loved his daughter very much and spoiled her blind. He hid absolutely nothing from her. So, when one day she pleaded with him to reveal to her the secret that enabled land mortals to breathe underwater, he agreed. That was only after he made her solemnly swear not to the tell the secret to any land mortal.

"Sadly, the young mermaid did not keep her promise. After charming a sailor, she revealed to him the secret of how to breathe underwater. When her father learned about this, he was furious and the other lords even more so. They held a meeting to decide what to do with the sailor. Finally, they all agreed the land mortal should never be allowed to leave the undersea world. They feared he might reveal the secret to other land mortals.

"In any case, they didn't have to worry because the sailor quickly adapted to living in the sea. He became so happy he never even considered a return to his own world. He got on well with the sea dwellers and became like them in many ways.

"However, as time passed, he slowly began to seek power, claiming he was superior to any sea creature. He was offered the rank of a lord, but he refused it. He wanted to be the supreme ruler, king of the undersea world. The Lords had no option but to banish him to a remote part of the sea.

"But the story doesn't end here," said Periwinkle. "This sailor never relinquished his ambitions for power, so he resorted to sorcery. With the help of a wicked nymph, he mastered the art of witchcraft and became a powerful wizard. Ever since, he has been plaguing us with numerous evil deeds, which even the lords are finding hard to ward off. And now, he cast a spell on our dear queen. She is in a very deep coma, and if she doesn't wake soon, she may even die, and with her death all harmony and balance in the seas shall be lost. However, the spell can be broken, and that's where we're hoping you can help us," finished Periwinkle.

"How?" asked Marissa. "And why me?"

"I'll explain," replied Periwinkle. "There is a rare, Anubias flower called the Neptius. It's the only known thing that can break the spell. We want you to pick this flower."

"Is that it?" frowned Marissa, baffled. "If it's so simple, why can't one of you sea creatures pick this flower?"

"It wouldn't work I'm afraid," Periwinkle informed her. "The spell was cast by a land mortal, so the flower has to be picked by a land mortal for the spell to be broken."

"I see," nodded Marissa, although she looked even more confused. "Very well. Where do I find this flower?"

"Ah, that's the snag," sighed Periwinkle. "Nobody knows where it is, except Fernando. Oh, that's the Wizard's name."

"Fernando?" Marissa almost laughed. "That doesn't sound like a great name for a powerful wizard! But never mind. Where do I find *him*?"

"That will be your first task," replied Periwinkle.

"And when or *if* I find him," asked Marissa, "how do I persuade him to tell me where the Neptius is?"

"That will be your second task," Periwinkle told her.

"Ah, there's the Palace!" broke in Delta.

Periwinkle was glad for the interruption.

CHAPTER FOUR

Straining her eyes, Marissa saw no palace of any sort. All she could see were tiny colorful lights shimmering in the distance like beacons in a misty night. She half expected to see a palace, similar to those in fairy tales with high towers and pointed turrets and pennants floating jauntily on top.

Eventually when the Palace came into view, Marissa saw it was nothing like that. As large as a football ground, it was dome-shaped and made entirely of glass, and not ordinary smooth glass but rather like crystal with a honeycomb pattern. It was tinged light green, the color of the sea, hence the reason why Marissa could not see in at first. What she had thought to be lights were in fact large pearls. The whole palace was encrusted with millions of them. Almost as big as golf balls, they shone and gleamed with every color of the rainbow.

"Wow!" gasped Marissa, awe-struck by the wondrous sight in front of her eyes. "I've never seen anything so beautiful!"

"Thank you," said Delta, flattered.

Presently, the sound of a horn echoed from within the Palace and an arched double door opened outwardly with barely any noise. Two Royal Guards stood on either side of it. They both saluted with their fins. Tarak did likewise as he led the procession through a long corridor. On either side were many recesses of various sizes and shapes. These were adorned with ornaments depicting strange sea creatures which Marissa did not recognize. They must have been made out of precious stones the way they sparkled and scintillated.

Unlike the outside of the Palace, the inside was made from smooth glass. The floor was paved emerald-green and the walls were decorated with gaudy tiles, similar to a mosaic bearing complex patterns.

Marissa noticed it was brighter inside, although she could see no apparent source of lighting. However, as she happened to look up, she saw why. All along the high, arched ceiling were what looked like crystal balls as large as her head. They shone very brightly, but strangely enough cast no shadows.

The long corridor ended in a T-junction and here Tarak stopped.

"You may dismiss," he said to the escort, and they at once left. "Please, step down," he told Marissa. He spoke politely enough but Marissa detected a hint of authority, and she complied. *Bossy, aren't we?* she felt like saying.

Without a word, Tarak led the way, taking the opposite way the escort had gone.

Marissa tried to walk normally as she did on land, but it was not easy. Every time her feet touched the ground, she floated upwards. It never occurred to her to just swim. However, after persisting for a while she managed to stay up on her feet. It was quite tiring though. She preferred to ride Delta.

After going through a couple more corridors, the small party came to a vast circular courtyard. Set around it were glass benches, semi-circular and tinged with different colors. Most of them were occupied by mermen and mermaids. Marissa noticed how sad and listless they looked. They merely glanced at her, their faces hardly showing any surprise. She was quite disappointed, expecting to be received as a heroine who had come to save their Queen. She was about to point that out to Periwinkle and Delta—then decided not to.

Tarak took a left turn and led the small party through a tunnel-like corridor which spiraled upwards. The higher they climbed the narrower the spiral became until they came to an arched double door in front of which stood two Royal Guards. Pushing the door open, they allowed the small party to go through.

A wave of apprehension swept over Marissa as soon as she found herself in a vast room. Circular, it was about half the size of the courtyard. It must have been right at the top of the palace, she guessed.

Delta remained by the entrance while Tarak conducted Marissa to the center of the room.

"Please, remain here," he said with his usual polite coldness, and before Marissa could say anything, he returned to join Delta by the entrance.

"What am I supposed to do?" she whispered to Periwinkle in a quavering voice. The seashell had been quiet all this time.

"Just relax," he told her, somehow detecting Marissa's nervousness. "You are in the Council Chamber. All matters are debated and decided here. Normally they are presided over by the Queen herself. Sadly, as you already know, she won't be present."

"Sorry," said Marissa. "I would love to have met her."

"You may still," said Periwinkle. "If all goes well that is."

"You mean it all depends on me." Marissa said as she smiled.

"Well, yes, mostly," said Periwinkle. "There are, of course, other things to consider."

Marissa did not pursue the matter. Instead, she glanced around and noticed for the first time Royal Guards all around the room. They looked vigilant and alert, ready for action if required. Across from the entrance was a semi-circular dais about two feet high. Set on top were glass chairs with raised arms and backs like thrones. Marissa counted them—there were fifteen in all. The middle one was slightly bigger and much higher. Marissa guessed it was the Queen's throne. It was tinged a deep blue; the others were emerald-green. Presently the dull sound of a gong echoed from somewhere in the room. A door on the left side opened and out came seven mermen, one behind the other. They were slightly bigger than the ones Marissa had seen so far. They looked powerful and impressive with muscular arms and chests. Just like the mermaids, they resembled one another with curly, blonde hair, dark blue eyes, and skin the color of burnished bronze.

Marissa could only stare at them with her mouth open. Before she could get over her surprise, the gong echoed once more and this time a door on the right side of the room opened.

Marissa gasped loudly—awe mingled with fear suddenly overwhelmed her. The creatures that came out must have been seven feet tall she guessed. Although shaped like humans, they looked nothing like them. Their skin was scaled more like a lizard rather than a fish. Their large hands and feet were webbed, the latter looked more like flippers. Their huge eyes were round and glassy and protruded like those of a chameleon. Their ears were shaped like seashells. Their mouths were crescent-shaped and lipless. As for noses, all Marissa could see were two holes for nostrils. *Gosh What are they?* she thought to herself.

As though reading her mind, Periwinkle whispered, "They are the Orgons. Please, don't be afraid."

But that was not easy. Trembling a little Marissa

watched as the Orgons filled the throne-like chairs on the right.

There was a long moment's silence. Marissa felt uncomfortable as both lords and Orgons studied her for quite some time. *Please, stop staring at me!* she felt like saying—but of course she wouldn't dare!

At last, one of the Orgons spoke, "Welcome, land maid. You know why you are here?" He spoke with a metallic voice that seemed to resonate like an echo.

Marissa understood every single word quite clearly. But all she could do was nod.

"Er-hum," went Periwinkle, as he cleared his throat.

"Er, yes, Sir!" replied Marissa, not knowing how to address the Orgon. "Periwinkle informed me earlier, Sir."

"Who is Periwinkle?" enquired one of the lords.

"I beg your pardon, my lord," chimed in Periwinkle. "She's referring to me. That's the name I assumed during my task."

Both lords and Orgons exchanged puzzled looks.

"Very well," said another Orgon. "Since you know why you are here, are you willing to help us?"

"You mean I have a choice?" asked Marissa.

"Certainly," replied one of the lords. "It's entirely up to you. But you must decide now—time is short!"

"Indeed, it is!" added an Orgon.

Marissa thought for a moment. She then sighed and said, "Very well. I shall do my best to help you. That's what my math teacher always tells me, 'Just do your best, Marissa.'"

The Lords and Orgons didn't seem to hear the last bit as they began to confer with one another quite audibly. They did that for a few minutes, then one of the Orgons who sat at the right-hand side of the Queen's throne stood up. He must be a senior one, guessed Marissa.

"You are very brave, young land maid," he said. "We thank you deeply. However, let me say this. Your task could prove hazardous. In fact, it will most likely be. Even your own life could be at risk. Do you still wish to go on with the task? Please think carefully."

Marissa perhaps should've said, *Well, nobody told me that before!* But again she didn't. She wasn't even angry. Surprising even herself, she replied, "Yes, I do, Sir." She smiled confidently, adding. "You say time is short. Hadn't I better start at once?"

"I believe you are right," agreed the senior Orgon. "This mission is a secret one, so the parties involved must be kept to a minimum. Tarak will accompany you with a team of royal guards. And, of course, you need transportation. Preferably the same dolphin that has bought you here?" At the back of the room Delta smiled with delight. "You shall be escorted to the Dark Zone and not beyond. The escort is then to return to the Palace. Chosen, please see that these instructions are carried out."

"Of course," replied Periwinkle.

"You may leave at once," continued the senior Orgon. "Land maid, thank you once more for offering to help. We wish you all a safe journey and a successful quest!" And so saying, he sat down.

"Thank you, Sir," said Marissa, curtseying politely.

"You did very well," whispered Periwinkle, not concealing his delight.

"You're a big liar, aren't you?" scolded Marissa, smiling at the same time. "Chosen!" she added sarcastically.

CHAPTER FIVE

Upon leaving the Council Chamber, Marissa resumed her comfortable seat on Delta's back. With Tarak leading, they left the Palace almost unnoticed. Already a dozen Royal Guards were waiting outside. Marissa couldn't tell if they were the same ones who had escorted them before because they all looked the same to her.

Tarak was a fish of a few words, Marissa found. With the wave of a fin and a stern look on his face he ordered the Royal Guards to resume their former position. Once more they divided into two single files and placed themselves along each side of Delta.

As before, the sound of a horn echoed. The Palace's doors closed silently, and the procession led by Tarak was on its way.

"Here we go," thought Marissa. "The true adventure has begun!"

The pace was fast. Soon the Palace dwindled behind them to become almost invisible. Only the shimmering of its thousands of pearls betrayed its whereabouts.

Marissa began to think back, wondering why she had agreed to help. She had the choice, and she could have easily refused. The Lords and Orgons spoke to her kindly and never put her under pressure. Had it been the opposite, she would have refused. Marissa could be very stubborn indeed. She glanced at Periwinkle clutched in her hand. He was her life support, literally. Of course, he had lied to her and tricked her, but she could understand his reasons for doing so. It *was* a matter of life or death as he had put it. She certainly didn't hold any bad feeling towards him. In fact, she had grown to be fond of him. Marissa smiled. *How could one like a seashell—that is, as one would like a living creature? Does he have feelings and emotions? And why is he referred to as the Chosen?* she wondered, and not for the first time. "Oh, well," she uttered quietly, "an adventure needs a mystery."

"How far is the Dark Zone?" she asked. She could not tell how far they had travelled, nor how long. Time and distance in the undersea world seemed strangely different from land.

"We still have a long way to go," answered Periwinkle.

"Why is it called the Dark Zone?" Marissa wanted to know. "Is it really dark?

"Yes, you could say that," said Delta. "What's more,

it's a cold and hostile place. It's a refuge for the lawless and the unscrupulous. There you'll find thieves, cut-throats, kidnappers, pirates, sorcerers... All in all, it's a very dangerous place!" he finished dramatically.

"That's just charming!" said Marissa, forcing a laugh. "Do we have to go through it? I mean is there a different route to wherever we're going?"

"Actually, we're not going anywhere in particular," informed Periwinkle. "Because we don't know where the Neptius is. Our goal is to find Fernando the Wizard, being the only one who can lead us to the flower. No doubt he has friends in the Dark Zone. They're just the sort of company he would mix up with."

"You mean they might tell us where we can find Fernando?" interrupted Marissa, almost sarcastically.

"I doubt it very much," said Periwinkle. "But you see we're going to look conspicuous in the Dark Zone—especially with you. News spreads fast there, and the Wizard should soon know about our presence. I'm sure he'll be interested in meeting a maid from his own world. Well, if he finds us, it's as good as us finding him!"

"I see," said Marissa thoughtfully. She was about to add, *So, you're going to use me as a bait!* But she refrained from doing so. It was too late now and there was no going back. Marissa knew this. She thought she had better take her adventure seriously. Her own life could be at risk. The Lords and Orgons had already warned her.

"Sir!" called a Royal Guard from the back, so suddenly

that Tarak stopped abruptly, and Delta almost bumped into him.

"What is it?" demanded the officer.

"I think we're being followed," replied the Royal Guard.

"Are you sure, Tion?" asked Tarak.

"Yes Sir, I believe so," replied Tion.

Tarak twiddled his beard thoughtfully, as if debating what initiative to take.

"We can't take any risks," said Periwinkle. "Whoever is following us must be caught and questioned."

Tarak nodded in agreement. "Let's swim on so as not to arouse suspicion. I have a plan." And they quickly left.

After a distance of a hundred yards or so the ground began to slope upwards, forming a steep hill. Once they were on the other side Tarak acted promptly.

"Tion, Shor," he ordered. "You remain behind. Find a place to hide and make sure our follower doesn't get away. Hurry up!" The Royal Guards acknowledged the order, and quickly swam off in opposite directions. "The rest will follow me. Let's go!"

They left at a quick pace. They soon came across another hill, higher and steeper than the first, and they stopped there.

"We'll wait here," said Tarak. "Let's hope Tion and Shor will not come back empty handed."

So, they waited. A long time elapsed. Everyone felt restless. The tension grew with every passing minute.

"Officer Tarak." It was Periwinkle. "I suggest you send someone to check on what's going on. We can't delay any longer, time is pressing."

However, there was no need, for just then Tion and Shor appeared over the crest of the hill. They were not alone. Sandwiched between them was a young mermaid. She held a small harp in her hands. Entwined in her golden hair were red and pink lily-shaped flowers. Marissa recognized her straight away. She was the first mermaid she had seen—singing and playing the harp.

Tion and Shor conducted the young mermaid towards Tarak. She looked calm and unscared. She even managed to smile at Marissa as she passed her. From close-up the young mermaid looked even more astonishingly beautiful.

Tarak studied the captive carefully before he spoke. "Was she alone?" he asked Tion and Shor.

"Yes, I was alone," replied the mermaid boldly.

"Silence!" snapped Tarak. "You speak when you're spoken to!"

The mermaid tossed her hair, a gesture of pride and defiance.

"What is your name?" demanded Tarak, seething.

"Elga."

"Why were you following us?"

"I wish to join you to search for the Neptius. I may be able to help."

Tarak frowned, taken aback. He was almost

speechless. "How did you…" he began, but he didn't finish.

"How do you know about the Neptius?" Periwinkle spoke up this time. "And our mission?"

Elga didn't seem surprised that Periwinkle had spoken.

"Answer!" shouted Tarak, finding his voice. "Who told you?"

Elga didn't seem fazed by the officer's outburst.

"I just know," she shrugged nonchalantly. "Anyway, I have close friends in the Palace. And I'm certainly not telling you who they are."

"We'll see about that!" fumed Tarak, glaring menacingly at the young mermaid.

"Just a moment," intervened Periwinkle. "Wouldn't be better if we allowed her to come with us? This way at least we can keep an eye on her. Besides," he added, "she actually may be able to help."

"Out of the question!" refused Tarak, adamantly. "I have a duty to perform. I cannot allow anyone that might jeopardize the success of this mission. The Council would never approve."

Periwinkle knew Tarak was right. "Very well," he conceded. "Then the young mermaid must be taken back to the Palace."

"And there she must remain," added Tarak, "until this mission is over."

Elga protested angrily, but to no avail. Tion and Shor were already taking her away. Marissa could still hear her protesting noisily until they vanished out of sight. What a shame, she thought. She liked Elga very much. She certainly had character!

Glancing round, Marissa noticed their surroundings were gradually changing. Everything was becoming darker—the rocks, sand, sea-weeds... The water itself had lost its sparkle. Now it looked murky and gloomy. For the first time, Marissa felt cold, and she started to shiver.

Just then Tarak came to a halt.

"Your duty ends here," he told the escort. "You may return to the Palace. Report to the Council that we have reached the Dark Zone safely."

He saluted in his usual manner. The Royal Guards did likewise, and they departed.

"So, we're in the Dark Zone at last," said Marissa.

"Only on the outskirts," corrected Periwinkle. "We should be there shortly."

"I already don't like this place," said Delta in a shaky voice. "It gives me the creeps. I wish the escort hadn't left!"

Marissa felt exactly the same.

CHAPTER SIX

"We're approaching the Dark Zone," announced Tarak, although there was no need for saying so. Everyone could see that.

Squinting through the murky water Marissa was just able to see the shapes of what appeared to be mountains. Craggy and much darker than their surroundings, they were a sinister and ominous sight to behold.

"Oh, no," groaned Delta, and Marissa could feel his body shaking.

"Silence!" ordered Tarak, glaring at the dolphin. "Everyone, keep your eyes and ears open!"

Marissa noticed the mountains were shaped very much like pyramids. They didn't look natural to her at all. Perhaps, she thought, they were carved by some giant creatures of the deep sea. Possibly eons ago. Between them they formed numerous, intricate gorges—some deep and wide, others narrow and shallow.

Tall, dark peaks loomed broodingly over the small party as they entered the Dark Zone through a deep chasm. Marissa felt a cold shiver run her spine. *This is really a creepy place,* she thought. Glancing left and right, she began to notice strange things going on. Dark shadows flitted furtively about, silent as ghosts. Eyes glowed like ember in crags and recesses, blinking and winking. Marissa was sure she could hear some whispering and rasping emanating from unseen places. Or was it just her imagination? She wondered if the others had also noticed what was going on around them. But she dared not ask.

Deeper and deeper, they plunged into the Dark Zone, winding their way through a maze of inexhaustible gorges. The pyramid-like mountains stood blacker and more foreboding than ever, giving Marissa a claustrophobic feeling. The trek seemed endless, and she wished something would happen. Her wish came true sooner than she had expected.

All of a sudden Tarak stopped, looking alert and concerned. "I think we may have company," he said, his voice a mere whisper. But they all heard him.

Marissa looked around, but all she could see was darkness. Then gradually, vague shadows began to appear all around them like wraiths. Slowly they took solid forms until the small party was completely surrounded.

"It's One-Eyed!" cried Delta, looking horrified. "Let's get out of here! Nowww!"

Tarak waved a fin to quiet him down. The dolphin shut up, but he couldn't stop shaking.

"The scoundrel," muttered Periwinkle. "As usual he has a band of renegades with him."

Marissa soon realized they were a referring to a large, fierce-looking tiger shark. He wore a black patch over one eye, hence the name One-Eyed. With him were another two tiger sharks, just as big and fierce. There was also a giant octopus, a huge eel, a horned sea-snake the size of a rock-python, three or four enormous spiky fishes with dagger-like teeth, and a number of horrible creatures encountered only in nightmares. Marissa felt her skin crawl and shivered.

"What have we here?" smirked One-Eyed as he came swaggering to meet Tarak. "Ha! I thought as much! Officer Tarak, isn't it? I remember you well. You arrested me once. I spent five years in jail on your account. How could I forget?"

Tarak hadn't forgotten either. But he deemed it wise to remain silent lest he might incur more trouble. However, he remained on his guard just in case One-Eyed were to try anything.

"What brought you here then?" sneered One-Eyed. "Not to arrest me again, I hope. Ha, ha! As if you could." He suddenly broke off when he noticed Marissa. "Well, well, well," he said, coming closer to her. "And what's this? A maid from the land? Ho, ho!" he laughed. "This is *really* interesting!"

Marissa gulped uncomfortably and said nothing.

45

One-Eyed glared at her, cocking his head to one side. "And what brings you here, my lovely? Hey? Well, speak up, land maid! I'm not a patient fish, you know... Answer me!"

"None of your business!" retorted Marissa. She was scared but tried not to show it.

"I'll make it my business!" snarled One-Eyed. "Now speak up!

Then Marissa did a crazy thing. She kicked One-Eyed right on the nose. *Smack!* She knew she might regret it, but she didn't care.

One-Eyed adjusted his eye patch which had slipped off position. If he was angry, he did not show it.

"Mm, plucky, aren't you?" he grinned, baring dagger-like teeth "I like that. But you still haven't answered my question."

"The land maid is a special guest of Her Majesty the Queen." It was Tarak who had spoken, but he didn't sound convincing. "You harm her, and you will be in dire trouble!"

"You are in no position to threaten me, Tarak!" snapped One-Eyed. "And isn't the Queen dead yet?"

"Of course not!" said Delta, finding his courage as well. "She lives, so there!"

"That's besides the matter," said One-Eyed. "I'm only interested in the land maid. I'll make a deal with you, Tarak. I will allow you to leave here unharmed, but the land maid will stay."

"No deal," refused Tarak. "It's my duty to protect the land maid and I shall do so at any cost."

"Have it your way then," warned One-Eyed. "Long-Arms!" he called. "Remove him and get the land maid!"

Immediately a giant octopus advanced towards Tarak. With a huge tentacle, he swept him to one side. But the senior Royal Guard was no push over. Recovering quickly, he lunged at Long-Arms who was not quick enough to parry the attack. Tarak sank his teeth in one of his tentacles. The giant octopus howled with pain. He thrashed his injured tentacle about wildly and uncontrollably. In doing so, he caught One-Eyed almost in the same place Marissa had kicked him.

"You clumsy idiot!" shouted the furious shark. "Watch what you're doing! I'll have that tentacle for lunch!"

Long-Arms was in too much pain to take notice of the threat. Not only that, he also created havoc among the other creatures. Everyone was trying to get out of his way. Most of them didn't manage to do so. All the time, One-Eyed was screaming his head off at the thrashing octopus.

"Quickly," urged Tarak, taking advantage of the confusion. "Let's get out of here."

They did not hang about. They slipped away unchallenged.

"They're escaping!" yelled One-Eyed in a fit of temper. "After them! I want the land maid alive. Kill the others!"

"Which way did they go?" asked a shark.

"This way I think!" said a horned sea-snake.

"No, that way!" corrected a giant eel.

They couldn't agree among themselves, and a heated

argument followed. It was utter chaos!

"Stop it, you imbeciles!" screamed One-Eyed, trying to bring some order. It took him a while to do so. "Follow me!" he ordered. "We'll soon catch up with them!"

A wild, frantic chase began through the numerous interlacing gorges. One-Eyed and his band of renegades had the advantage because they knew the Dark Zone like you would know your back garden. It was their home ground. Taking one short-cut after another, they soon caught up with the small party.

Marissa kept glancing back. Each time she did so, she saw the pursuers were closing on them.

"They're not far behind!" she warned. "Can we go any faster?"

"I'm doing my best!" panted Delta.

"Let's keep going!" urged Tarak. "We'll try and lose them again. This way!""

He suddenly swerved into a narrow channel. There was just enough room for them to swim through.

One-Eyed and his gang tried to follow but there wasn't enough space for all of them. In fact, Long-Arms got stuck, and the rest had to take a detour.

The chase went on. It became a game of cat-and-mouse. The pursuers would disappear for a while and then reappear somewhere else.

"We can't go on like this forever!" complained Delta, exhausted. "Chosen, what do we do?"

"They've caught up with us again!" cried Marissa

before Periwinkle could answer.

They were going through a wide, deep ravine when suddenly a gigantic shape materialized in front of them. It was far too big for a ray fish like the one Marissa had seen before. It was much, much bigger! The monstrous creature glided above them and headed towards One-Eyed and his gang.

The small party stopped to watch, surprised and relieved at the same time.

"Look!" laughed Marissa, delighted. "It's chasing One-Eyed and his gang! Whatever is it?"

"It's only Sept," replied a voice. "A friendly monster."

CHAPTER SEVEN

"Elga! I thought…" began Marissa, then she stopped, lost for words. "Anyway, I'm sure glad to see you!" she managed to say at last.

"Me too!" added Delta, still shaking, but this time with delight.

Tarak, on the other hand, did not look pleased. "Perhaps you can explain your presence here," he said, with a stern look on his face. "How come you're not back in the palace? And what happened to Tion and Shor?"

"Oh, them," smiled Elga. "I guess they're back in the Palace. I've never seen anyone swim so fast!"

"This is no time for pleasantry!" rebuked Tarak. "I need an explanation—now!"

"Just tell us what happened," intervened Periwinkle gently. "Please, Elga, go ahead."

"Well, it's quite simple really," began Elga. "I was angry and disappointed that I wasn't allowed to join you. I wanted to so much. Of course, I didn't want to go back to the Palace. And, I had to somehow get rid of my escort, that is Tion and Shor. So, I began to play a special tune on my harp intended for my friend Sept."

"You mean," interrupted Marissa, "that huge creature that came to our help? What is it, anyway?"

"An orlog," explained Elga. "It's a rare sea monster who loves music. If played properly that is. That's how I charmed Sept a long time ago."

"Just get to the point!" said Tarak impatiently. "You call that a simple explanation?"

"You ought to guess what happened," retorted Elga. "I called Sept and he came to my rescue. Is that simple enough for you?"

Marissa smiled. She could just imagine Sept chasing Tion and Shor. They must have been scared out of their wits. She didn't blame them for running away.

"And I assume," concluded Tarak, "you've been following since. With your friend, Sept, of course" he added with a touch of sarcasm.

"That's right," replied Elga. "Then when I saw you were in trouble, I sent Sept to help you."

"Thank you," said Marissa, gratefully. "We don't know what would've happened to us without your help."

"You sure came at the right time," Delta said while beaming.

"You certainly did," agreed Periwinkle. "Officer Tarak, I suggest we allow Elga to join us. She may be able to help again. Her friend Sept will be a great asset to us. The success of our task is crucial."

Even Tarak saw the sense in that. But he did not admit it straight away. He was silent for a long moment, twiddling his beard, trying to think of a way to argue the point. In the end he gave up.

"Very well," he muttered moodily. "She may come." He then glared at Elga. "But I'm warning you. This is not going to be a picnic party. I'm in charge of this mission. You just do as I…"

"I'll do as you say," cut in Elga. "Promise."

"That settles it then," smiled Marissa, delighted that Elga had at last joined them.

"I'll just call Sept then," said Elga.

Tarak was going to object once more. But the young mermaid had already started playing the harp. It was a jolly melody, played in high notes, and it was fast and rhythmical, which made Marissa want to dance. Even Delta could not help wriggling his body and flapping his tail to the beat of music. Elga too was moving her head from side to side as she plucked the harp.

This went on for quite a while with Tarak staring at them in disbelief. At last he exploded. "This is not a merry party!" He had to shout to make himself heard. "This is ridiculous! Chosen, please. This is madness!"

"Look, there he is!" cried Marissa when she saw Sept

gliding towards them through the dark waters.

"What took him so long?" muttered Tarak.

"He was probably having fun chasing One-Eyed and his gang," joked Delta.

"Oh, Sept loves chasing," said Elga. "He's so playful—and very friendly. But not everyone knows that."

When Sept came closer, Marissa saw how huge he was. He must have been the size of a double-decker bus, or even bigger. He looked similar to a dragon, but instead of wings he had large flippers. His tail was quite long and arrow-tipped. He had two horns on his head, short but sharp. His body was covered with green and yellow scales, and his face was quite friendly with big round eyes and a smiling mouth.

"Hello, Sept!" greeted Elga, fussily stroking his head. "Did you have fun?"

Sept nodded his head two or three times. His eyes grew bigger and his nostrils flared to show that he did have a good time.

"Good!" smiled Elga. "Now I would like you to meet some of my friends."

"Do we have to go through this?" snarled Tarak, not hiding his annoyance.

No one took notice of him.

"Pleased to meet you, Sept," said Marissa.

"Hello!" said Delta.

Sept kept nodding his head.

"Sept can't speak," explained Elga. "But he

understands everything you say."

"Now that the introduction is over," said Tarak, "let's move on. We are wasting precious time."

"Yes, we had better," agreed Periwinkle.

They did not tarry any longer. With Tarak leading once more, the small party was on its way. Elga swam alongside Delta so she could chat with Marissa. Sept followed at the back, a slight distance away.

Having never seen a land mortal before Elga showed great interest in Marissa. She started asking her all sorts of questions, first about Marissa herself then about the land and its people and how they lived. Marissa was only too glad to answer the mermaid's questions, although at times she found it hard to explain to her technical things such as computers and mobile phones. All the same, Elga listened eagerly with fascination. Then it was her turn to tell Marissa about her world and Marissa was just as fascinated. They chatted and laughed together like two old school friends who had just met after the summer holiday, and they had plenty to tell each other.

"I must confess to something," said Elga, looking somewhat embarrassed.

"What is it?" asked Marissa, curious.

"I…" Elga hesitated for a moment. Then went on, "You see…I'm related to the mermaid who charmed Fernando the Wizard. I feel guilty about the whole thing. I mean if that didn't happen, then the Queen would've been all right now."

"But that happened a long time ago," Marissa told her. "You shouldn't feel guilty about it. It's not your fault."

"Maybe not," sighed Elga. "But I can't help feeling so. That's why I wanted so much to join you. I would do anything to help."

"You already have done so," Marissa reminded her. "You know, Sept?"

"Oh, that was nothing." Elga smiled faintly, but still looked sad.

"What's done is done," said Periwinkle soothingly. "But let's keep this to ourselves for now."

"Humph!" grunted Tarak who had obviously been listening too. "You should feel guilty and rightly so. And we don't need help from the likes of you."

"That's not fair!" shouted Marissa angrily. "You're just a big bully, so shut up!"

Tarak must have been furious at being spoken to in such a manner. But, surprisingly, he did not say or do anything.

Besides something began to happen. At first, there was just a slight disturbance in the water. They all started bobbing up and down, gently at first then faster and faster.

"W-what is it?" asked Marissa, her voice quavering.

"Just a tremor," Periwinkle reassured her. "It can cause a disturbance in the water. Not to worry, it will soon pass."

It was quite the opposite. The turbulences grew stronger and stronger—so much so that Marissa could hardly sit still on Delta. They both rocked up and down.

"This is getting worse!" cried Marissa, shaking violently.

"I don't like this at all!" added Delta.

Even Tarak looked concerned. He glared at Elga as if she were to blame.

"Don't look at me like that!" Elga shouted angrily.

"Just keep calm, all of you," said Periwinkle, strangely enough his voice unaffected.

But this wasn't easy to do.

While this was going on Marissa could hear a rumbling noise. Only then did she notice that the mountains themselves were shaking terribly. She had never felt so scared in her whole life. Not only that, she was finding it hard to stay on Delta's back. Suddenly she slipped off and in doing so she instinctively tried to grab one of the dolphin's fins with the hand holding Periwinkle.

"No!" Periwinkle tried to warn.

Marissa quickly realized her mistake—but too late.

"Blurb! Blurb! Blurb!" she went, frantically thrashing about.

She could no longer breathe underwater.

CHAPTER EIGHT

With bulging eyes, Marissa watched Periwinkle float away from her. Soon he vanished out of sight.

"Mmm! Mmmmmm!" Marissa tried to attract the attention of Elga, pointing in Periwinkle's direction.

The mermaid quickly saw what Marissa was trying to say. As fast as she could, she darted through the murky water in the direction Marissa had pointed. The ground and mountains were still shaking violently, but the brave mermaid took no heed of the falling rocks.

"Here! Here!" Elga heard Periwinkle shout, but where was he? With the terrible noise going on, she couldn't really tell. She then noticed something flashing brightly to her right, on and off. "Here!" she heard again.

At last, Elga spotted the seashell who was still flashing on and off. She swiftly swam towards him.

"Hurry!" said Periwinkle as the mermaid had him safely in her hand. "Or the land maid will die!" But the mermaid needed no urging. She was already swimming back as fast as she could.

Just then everything became still and silent. The mountains stopped shaking—the water quivered no more.

Meanwhile Marissa was on the verge of passing out. Her face had turned blue from lack of oxygen. She couldn't hold her breath any longer.

"Please, please, hold on!" begged Delta, panicking. It was too late to swim to the surface for air. He would never make it there in time.

Tarak paced to and fro, muttering to himself as usual. Delta nearly told him to be quiet, but he was too worried to bother.

"Here she comes!" he cried jubilantly when he saw Elga swimming towards them.

***

"It's all right, Marissa," said Periwinkle. "You can breathe now. You've got me back!"

But all Marissa could hear were faint, bubbly sounds which she could not make sense of. And her vision was blurred. When she realized she had Periwinkle back in her hand, she clasped him tighter, as if afraid he might get away from her again. She then began to breathe deeply. Gradually the color returned to her face; the dizziness cleared from her head and at last she was able to focus again. Surprisingly enough it was Tarak who spoke first.

"Are you all right?" he asked, looking quite concerned.

Marissa could only nod.

"Phew!" said Delta, breathing a sigh of relief. "For a moment, I thought we'd lost you!"

Marissa patted the dolphin's head. She then turned to Elga. "I don't know how to thank you. You saved my life!"

"Indeed, you have," agreed Periwinkle. "What's more, you risked your own life. That was very brave of you."

"It's all right," smiled Elga.

"What was that anyway?" asked Marissa. "An earthquake?"

"Probably," replied Tarak, not entirely sure himself.

"No, that wasn't natural," disagreed Delta. "I'd say witchcraft, that's what it was. I can feel it."

"Witchcraft?" frowned Marissa. "You mean the Wizard, Fernando?"

"Of course! Who else?" The dolphin sounded as if this was the most natural answer in the world. "He has the power!"

"Chosen?" enquired Tarak. "What do you think?"

"Delta could well be right," answered Periwinkle. "Perhaps Fernando had already found us."

"So where is he then?" asked Marissa.

"Yes," agreed Elga. "Why doesn't he show himself?"

Then Delta cried, "What's that? Look!"

Heading towards them was what looked like a sledge

drawn by some weird creatures. Riding in it was a skeletal figure which Marissa could not make out. But the nearer it came the more uneasy she felt. That could be said about the others too.

"I'll be…" began Tarak, as if he had seen the devil himself. "It's Shantaya!"

"Who is she?" Marissa wanted to know.

"It's a nymph," Elga informed her. "A wicked, evil nymph!"

"Some say she's immortal," added Delta in awe. "It was she who taught Fernando witchcraft. She must be hundreds of years old—much, much older than the Wizard himself. Needless to say, she's more powerful than he is."

"Things are getting better all the time," sighed Marissa. "Now what do we do?

"Nothing," whispered Periwinkle. "Let's wait and find out what Shantaya wants."

"Is that really wise?" moaned Delta. But no one took notice of him, their eyes riveted on the approaching sledge. Even Sept, who was at the back, looked entranced.

At last, the sledge came to an abrupt halt. The first thing that caught Marissa's eyes were the four creatures pulling it. They were as large as sea-lions and heavily scaled. A line of sharp spikes ran along their backs. They had only one eye in the middle of their foreheads and these glowed like embers. Long, upturned tusks protruded from their slavering jaws.

"Ugh!" went Marissa, grimacing with disgust.

"Whatever are they?"

"They're mollasks," whispered Elga. "They're vicious creatures!"

Still holding the reins with one hand Shantaya the Nymph at last stood up and Marissa was able to have a proper look at her. She was, more or less, the shape of a human, but her body looked like an elongated frog. Her arms and legs were also frog-like. Her head was oval-shaped and her eyes round and glassy. She had elfish, pointed ears, and her nose was ridiculously long which reminded Marissa of Pinocchio. Her mouth was small in contrast and almost lipless. The most ridiculous thing about her was her spiky hair—It was orange and purple and it stood up like the quills of a porcupine. *She would make a good punk rocker,* thought Marissa, giggling inwardly.

"So…" began the Nymph in a shrill, irksome voice, "This is quite a party!" And when no one said anything, she went on, "I think I can guess what you're up to. You're wasting your time. And you, land maid!" She pointed a long, ugly finger at Marissa. "I advise you to go back to your world. You can't fight me!"

Marissa frowned. *Does she think I'm a sort of witch?* she thought. But she remained silent.

"I could've already destroyed all of you," raved on Shantaya. "See how powerful I am!" And to prove so she began to chant some unintelligible words.

Almost at once the mountains began to shake, just like they had done before, but much more violently.

"So, it was *her* doing!" cried Delta above the noise. "And not Fernando as we'd thought!"

"It looks like it!" shouted Marissa. "Now we have to deal with both of them!"

Just then the mountains came to a standstill and the noise gradually died away.

"Hee, hee, hee!" cackled Shantaya. "Yes! I possess powers that no sea or land mortal can match! No one, you hear me!"

"We are all aware of your powers, Shantaya," said Tarak meekly, not wishing to provoke the nymph further. "However, we are not here to challenge you. Our business concerns Fernando. We wish to speak with him on urgent matters."

"Oh, do you?" sneered Shantaya. "So, it's that fool you wish to see. Mmm, I wonder why? Could it be perhaps concerning the Neptius? Very well, I shall take you to him. Come with me—all of you!" she ordered.

The four mollasks growled deeply to emphasize the command.

Just then something quite unexpected happened. For some reason, Sept decided to attack Shantaya. Snorting furiously, he lunged at the nymph.

"No, Sept, no!" warned Elga. "She'll hurt you!"

But the warning came too late.

Shantaya, half expecting the attack, pointed a finger at the charging Sept.

"You stupid monster!" she muttered. "Do you think

64

your size is going to help you? I think not!"

No one knew exactly what happened. There was a sudden, violent swirl of water that enveloped Sept, spinning him round and round, as if he were in a giant washing machine. This lasted only for half a moment. Everyone thought Sept had vanished altogether, but not so. He had simply shrunk to the size of a mouse.

"You're not so big now!" laughed the nymph. "Let this be a warning to all of you!"

"Oh no, Sept!" sobbed Elga, hugging the little creature. "Why did you do it?" But Sept only looked at her helplessly. Seething, the young mermaid yelled at the top of her voice, "You wicked nymph! What did you do to him!"

"Silence!" ordered Shantaya. "He's lucky to be still alive. Now all of you, come along with me, or you shall suffer the consequences. And I promise you, they won't be pleasant."

They believed her, so resignedly they did as told.

CHAPTER NINE

Their spirits dampened by the turn of events, the small party swam close together, each one wrapped up in their own thoughts.

Shantaya was certainly going to cause problems, mused Marissa. Anyone who could make mountains shake and reduce Sept to the size of a mouse would. *What did she want from them anyway?* Marissa asked herself. *And how does she know about the Neptius?*

Marissa still found it hard to believe that moments ago the tiny creature in Elga's hands was the size of a double-decker bus. She noticed how he kept trembling and whining like a new-born kitten. Elga huddled him closer to her, speaking soft words to him. That was all she could do to comfort the poor little creature.

Marissa wondered if Sept was going to stay that size for good. She felt sad for him. Moreover, he would be of no help to them as they had hoped and expected. Nothing appeared to be going right in their quest. Marissa doubted if they would ever succeed. What about the Queen? Would she die if they failed? That seemed more and more likely.

At last, they left the Dark Zone behind. But that didn't raise their spirits. The area they entered was barren and just as gloomy. Hardly anything grew here and what did looked sickly and pitiful. They could see no fishes or any other living creatures around. Everything was devoid of life. "Perhaps they should call this place the 'Dead Zone,'" whispered Marissa with a wry smile.

But the place was not quite dead. Unbeknown to Marissa and her companions they were being watched closely.

"Come on out, my lovelies!" Shantaya suddenly called. "Come and see what I have for you!"

At first no one knew what she was talking about. Then…

"Look!" cried Marissa, pointing. "It's those horrid creatures. What are they called again?"

"Mollasks," Elga told her. "They're mutants—a creation of Shantaya herself. She has experimented on many unfortunate creatures to make monsters out of them. That's her favorite hobby."

"Some sort of Dr Frankenstein, is she?" said Marissa, more to herself.

There must have been dozens of the mollasks. Now they came from everywhere, surrounding the small party. Their sole eyes glowed malevolently and their jaws dripped with gooey green saliva, with deep, rasping noises coming out of their throats.

"Come on out, all of you!" called Shantaya. "Don't be shy! Come and say hello!"

Just then a double headed shark appeared out of no-where. It was followed by a huge octopus with lobsters' legs instead of tentacles. After these came a triple-headed eel. Then a creepy, crab-like creature emerged from another side. Before long, they were surrounded by all sorts of hideous monstrosities encountered only in nightmares.

"Do you like what I've got for you?" laughed Shantaya. "But you're not having them yet. Later, later, I promise you!"

The mutant creatures seemed to be more interested in Marissa than anyone else. They stared and glared at her with hungry, baleful eyes. One or two came even closer to her for a better look. Marissa felt her skin crawl with fear and disgust. She half shut her eyes, expecting one of them to bite one of her legs off at any moment. She braced herself, wincing, wishing them to move away.

"Go now, my beauties," ordered Shantaya. "I shall bring them to you again very soon!"

Ghost-like, the mutants silently and mysteriously vanished, as if swallowed by the ground. Perhaps that was where they lived, thought Marissa, puzzled but relieved.

"Well good riddance!" she muttered, still trembling.

"Yes, but for how long?" added Delta gloomily.

"Sooner than you think!" snapped Shantaya, who

must have heard. "Now be quiet and let's move on. Home is not far away."

***

The Nymph's home turned out to be a huge beehive-shaped mountain. It must have been hundreds of feet high, Marissa guessed. Dotted all around it and all the way up to the top were numerous caves of different sizes and shapes. Most of them were in total darkness, but some were illuminated by dim lights. These were also of different colors—red, blue, orange... Marissa could hear some noises emanating from them. She heard pitiful moans and cries, as if in terrible agony, accompanied by clanging and the rattling of chains.

"Be silent, you miserable creatures!" shouted Shantaya. "You ought to be grateful to me! You will soon look and feel much better! You know my work is always excellent!"

"You wicked nymph!" Marissa couldn't hold her anger. "Why do you do such horrid things?"

"Horrid things?" sneered Shantaya. "How little you know! In any case, I'm not going to discuss my great work with an ignorant land maid. I have neither the time nor the patience." She paused briefly. "Or perhaps I will... hmmm... How would you like a fish tail instead of those silly long legs of yours? Yes, I can just see that!"

"No, thank you!" gasped Marissa, horrified.

"I shall have to think about that," grinned Shantaya.

70

"So, it's the Wizard you wish to see. Very well, then you shall see him!"

At the base of the mountain was a large round rock. The nymph pointed a finger towards it and mumbled some words. The rock shuddered for a moment then rolled over to one side, revealing the entrance to a cave.

"All of you inside there!" ordered Shantaya. "I shall deal with you shortly. I have other business to attend to for now!"

Before they entered the cave, the Nymph stopped them. "Just a moment. How come you can breathe underwater, land maid?"

Marissa's heart skipped a beat, but she quickly recovered. "I was told the secret, of course! How else would I be able to breathe underwater?"

Shantaya glared at her suspiciously. "What have you got in your hand? Show me!"

Marissa's heart must've skipped two beats this time.

"Oh, you mean this?" she laughed. "A seashell. Pretty, isn't it? You can have it if you want. Here. Take it!"

"Humph! As if I would!" snorted Shantaya, a contemptuous look on her face. "All of you inside!"

Somewhat relieved, they all entered the cave. The rock rumbled behind them to block the entrance once more.

Apprehensively Marissa gave a quick glance round. The cave was quite deep, she realized. It was illuminated by a dim light cast by a crystal ball on the ceiling. Crouched at the bottom of the cave was what Marissa guessed to be the Wizard, Fernando. He stirred and groaned, obviously he had been asleep and was just waking up. Sensing he had company, he slowly stood up. He rubbed the sleep off his eyes and peered through the dim light.

After a long silence, he spoke. "Who are you?" His voice was deep and croaky, almost inhuman.

Marissa took charge. "I'm a land maid. I'm called Marissa. These are my friends. You must be Fernando." Her voice shook a little.

"Yes, I am," was the reply.

"We were looking for you," Marissa told him.

"And we have found you!" added Delta unnecessarily.

"What do you want of me?" The Wizard sounded wary.

"It's a long story," Marissa told him. "But briefly, we urgently need your help."

"I don't know what you want, land maid. But whatever it is, you came too late."

Fernando came closer to Marissa who got off Delta's back. They both stood on the brightest spot of the cave. She had expected the Wizard to be tall and lanky with long white hair and a straggling beard like in fairy tales. She had imagined him to be wearing a grey robe and holding a crooked staff in one hand.

However, he looked nothing like that—quite the opposite. He was young, short and chubby. He had black hair and a well-trimmed beard, which surprised Marissa. She guessed he looked Spanish, or possibly Latino—perhaps because of his dark complexion. He wore a white shirt torn off at the elbows and black trousers reaching to his knees. Nothing on his feet, which to Marissa's surprise were slightly webbed. His hands were webbed too. A thick belt with a silver buckle supported his podgy stomach.

For a long time, Marissa and Fernando just stared at each other. Perhaps the Wizard looked the more surprised of the two.

"But you're human," he said at length. Despite the surprised look on his face, he appeared to be pleased.

"Yes," replied Marissa. "And so are you."

Fernando shook his head sadly. "I'm not sure anymore. I have lived in the undersea world for so long I now feel like one of its creatures. Never mind," he added. "It's too late now to do anything about it." He paused briefly, then asked, "What brought you here?"

"Well…you," said Marissa rather clumsily. "We need your help. Urgently!"

"Of course, the Neptius" he said, nodding thoughtfully. "It has to be picked by a land mortal to break the spell cast on the Queen." His head dropped with shame and guilt. "It was a terrible thing I had done, terrible. I regret it bitterly. If only I could help. Alas, I'm powerless. Like you I'm also a prisoner of Shantaya. I dare not imagine what she intends to do with us."

"She'll probably feed us to her mutants," muttered Delta from the back. "What are we going to do?"

"*I* know what to do!" Tarak suddenly cried. He

lunged at Fernando, butting him on the chest. The Wizard spun two or three times through the water and hit the back of the cave. He slumped to the ground, half unconscious.

Marissa was absolutely furious. "Are you mad?" she yelled.

"It's all because of him and that we are in this mess!" Tarak yelled back.

"Enough!" ordered Periwinkle. "This is not helping at all!"

Marissa and Tarak glared at each other, but said nothing.

Elga went to attend to Fernando.

"He's all right," she said. "Just slightly dazed."

Fernando groaned, holding his painful chest. "I don't blame you, Officer Tarak. I deserve worse." He obviously knew the senior royal guard.

"If the Queen should die," threatened Tarak. "I'll…"

"Just calm down!" interrupted Periwinkle. "What's done is done. Perhaps Fernando can redeem himself by helping us. Are you willing to do so?" he asked the Wizard.

"Yes, but how?" wailed Fernando. "Shantaya will never allow us to leave this cave. Before I was the only threat to her because I'm still considered to be a land mortal. But now there is you too," he told Marissa. "She will either get rid of us altogether or change us into some hideous monsters who will be her slaves forever. I don't know which is worse," he finished miserably.

"What's she up to anyway?" asked Marissa, curious.

"To rule the undersea world, of course," replied Fernando. "She has already a large army of renegades and hundreds of mutants. They are increasing every day. If something is not done soon, the whole sea kingdom will be at peril."

"But why did you side with Shantaya in the first place?" Marissa wanted to know.

"Because I too wanted to rule the undersea world," answered Fernando. "But to be able to do so, I needed magical powers and Shantaya gave them to me. When I became strong and powerful, she goaded me to put a spell on the Queen. Which I shamefully did. I was blinded by my ambitions then. I'm very, very sorry."

"Humph!" snorted Tarak scornfully. "Too late now for apologies!"

"I did try to redeem myself," continued Fernando. "But Shantaya realized that, knowing that I was the only one capable of breaking the spell cast on the Queen. So, to be on the safe side as far as she was concerned, she removed all the magical powers she had given me. And now, as you can see, I'm her captive just as you are."

"I don't believe any of that," remarked Tarak. "Why should we trust him? It's more than likely he's still in league with Shantaya!"

"We have no choice but to believe him," said Periwinkle. "For the time being at least. We shall take a step at a time. First how do we get out of here?"

CHAPTER TEN

Elga suddenly cried out, "Look! I think Sept is growing bigger. He is! He is!"

"Is he really?" cried Marissa, hardly believing her ears. But she didn't need an answer—she could see that Sept was already the size of a rabbit. And he was still growing before her very eyes.

"Oh, I'm so glad!" said Elga gleefully. "I was afraid he might stay small forever."

"So was I," said Marissa, just as happy.

Everyone watched in amazement as Sept slowly increased in size. Fernando looked the most surprised. Marissa had to explain to him what had happened when they encountered Shantaya the first time.

"I thought he looked like an orlog," he said. "But I wasn't sure because he was too small—even for a young one!"

Sept was now as large as a donkey, and still growing.

"The spell must've been only temporary," said Periwinkle. "The only trouble is, what will happen when Sept is back to his normal size?"

"That's right," agreed Marissa. "The cave is not big enough for all of us."

"We'll be utterly squashed!" wailed Delta.

"I wish we'd never brought him along with us!" complained Tarak. "You should've listened to me!"

"You don't have to worry," Elga told them. "Don't you see? When Sept is big enough, he would be able to move the rock. He's very strong."

"Yes, that's right," agreed Marissa.

"Let's see him do that then," said Tarak grumpily.

As if to take the challenge, Sept at once moved towards the rock and started pushing it with all his might. Again and again he tried, straining and pushing, but the rock wouldn't budge an inch.

"Maybe Shantaya put a spell on the rock," said Delta miserably. "Oh, what's the use? We'll never get out of here!" By now Sept had doubled in size and it was a bit of a squash in the cave.

"Keep going, Sept," encouraged Elga. "You can do it, but you must hurry!"

Sept seemed to understand the situation they were in. He doubled his efforts. He pushed and heaved and strained while everyone watched anxiously. At last, the rock budged a little.... Then a little bit more. There was a subdued cheer.

All of a sudden, the rock rolled to once side, as if on its own. Everyone gasped at the sight that greeted their eyes. It was Shantaya!

"Ha! Do you think you can escape me that easily?" she sneered. "Well, you're wrong!"

Actually, it was she who was wrong. Sept had grown so big that he desperately wanted to get out of the cave before he got stuck. He squeezed and squeezed himself through the entrance and came out the other side with a loud POP! In doing so he landed right on top of Shantaya

"Arggghhh!" she shrieked. "Helpppp!" But her voice was muffled on account of Sept sitting on top of her and so it did not carry far.

It was a perfect opportunity for the captives to escape.

***

They had covered a long distance and thankfully did not encounter any of the Nymph's monsters. However, they were still in her territory, and no one felt at ease. Marissa, who had resumed her seat on Delta's back, kept glancing back to see if they were being pursued. Not yet, but it wouldn't be long before Shantaya showed up. Her sledge was much faster than any of them.

Marissa hoped they would have enough time to reach the Neptius, wherever its location may be. She assumed Fernando was leading them there. He was right ahead, leading the group of escapees. He swam smoothly and faster than any human could. *But is he really human now?* Marissa wondered.

Just then a dark shape suddenly cut across their path. Fernando did not see it until it was too late. *Smash!* He collided with the dark shape, which Marissa recognized to be a giant ray fish. It was even bigger than the last one she had encountered. Knocked of his senses, the Wizard sank to the bottom of the sea like a sack of potatoes.

"Oh, no!" Marissa and Elga cried together.

"Why can't' they ever look where they're going?" complained Delta. "I told you they're a hazard!"

"Stupid, clumsy thing!" muttered Tarak, not exactly clear to whom he was referring—the ray fish or the Wizard.

It took some time before Fernando came to his senses again. Groggily he shook his head. He didn't seem to be aware of where he was or what had happened. One at a time, they tried to explain to him, but that only confused him even more.

"I have no idea what you're talking about," he said at last. "I can't remember anything. I don't even know who I am!"

"Who cares about you?" shouted Tarak. "The Neptius... You must remember where the Neptius is!"

"What's that?" asked Fernando, looking genuinely puzzled.

"It's a special flower," Marissa told him. "We urgently need it to save the Queen's life!"

"I never heard of such a thing," said Fernando,

shaking his dazed head. "I… I'm sorry… I can't help you."

"Leave it for now," suggested Periwinkle. "Give him a little more time—"

"Which we haven't got!" said Tarak. "Besides, how do we know he's not lying. Perhaps he's still in league with the Nymph!"

"Again, we have no choice but to believe him," said Periwinkle. "He could be telling the truth after all."

Tarak didn't look convinced, but said nothing.

"How come that seashell in your hand talks?" Fernando suddenly asked Marissa, looking puzzled.

"Oh," began Marissa, not sure how to explain. "I really don't know. Maybe because he's the *Chosen*? Whatever that means."

"I see," nodded Fernando, frowning deeply as if trying to remember something. "And you…" He was going to ask Marissa another question but changed his mind. "It doesn't matter," he said with a faint smile.

"Are we just going to hang around here," said Tarak, "and wait for Shantaya to show up?"

"That's true," agreed Marissa. "She can't be far by now."

"But where shall we go?" asked Delta.

"Anywhere," replied Periwinkle. "As far as possible. Let's hope Fernando will get his memory back soon."

"I'll bash his head in if he doesn't," threatened Tarak. "He'll remember all right!"

"There we go again," chided Marissa, tutting and

shaking her head. "Threats, threats and more threats! Is that all you can do?"

"Be careful, land maid, not to go too far," warned Tarak. "I shall not tolerate your insolence any longer."

Marissa was about to retaliate, but just then Elga started to play the harp and sing at the same time. At first the sweet melody seemed to calm everyone's nerves. But as the mermaid's voice rose together with the music she played, something began to happen to Fernando...

"No, please, no," he kept saying, shaking his head. "Please, stop. I don't want to hear that again. Please, stop!" He behaved as if he were having a nightmare, his hands pressed hard against his ears.

"Oh, I'm sorry," said Elga. "I just thought perhaps a bit of singing..."

"My ship! Where's my ship?" cried Fernando in a state of panic. "I must find my ship. I want to return to land. I must hurry!"

Then he was off, swimming frantically, thrashing about clumsily, not as smoothly as before.

"What's the matter with him?" frowned Marissa.

"He's gone mad!" fumed Tarak.

"It's all my fault," said Elga, looking guilty.

"Where's he off to anyway?" Delta wanted to know.

"We'd better find out," prompted Periwinkle. "Let's hurry before we lose sight of him!"

They soon spotted the Wizard. They could still hear him faintly, repeating the same words over and over again.

Finally, they caught up with him. They found him standing in front of an ancient galleon. It lay on its side with a gaping hole in its hull. Its masts were broken and its riggings were a tangled up mess. Its rusty guns stuck up like rotten, black teeth. Obviously, the ship had been engaged in a sea battle and had sunk as a result.

"It's too late now," moaned Fernando miserably. "I shall never return to land. What am I to do?"

No one could answer that or say anything to comfort him. They weren't even sure what he meant.

Was that really Fernando's ship? wondered Marissa. It must have been hundreds of years old. *And how old was Fernando for that matter?* She couldn't really guess.

"I'm sorry," apologized Fernando after a long, awkward silence. And when no one said anything, he went on, "I believe you wish to know where the Neptius is?"

"Do you remember where it is?" asked Marissa.

"Yes, of course," replied Fernando.

"Are you sure?" asked Delta. "I thought you lost your memory"

"Never mind," cut in Tarak sharply. "Just lead us on to it. We're running out of time!"

They moved on quickly with Fernando leading once more.

"I'm so pleased," Elga said smiling. "I was feeling bad about it."

"Don't be," Marissa smiled back. "It's thanks to you that he got his memory back. I mean your singing and playing the harp. I believe that's how he was charmed and lured into the undersea world a long time ago. Perhaps that jogged his memory a little."

"Oh, that," said Elga. "Strange, it was one of my ancestors who was responsible."

"That's all in the past now," Marissa told her soothingly. "Don't fret, I'm sure all will work out well. Once we have the Neptius and get back safely to the palace everything will be all right."

"I hope so," said Elga, more to herself. "I really do."

But was it going to be as simple as that? Just then something occurred to Marissa, which she hadn't thought about before. How long had she been in the undersea world? It seemed a long time. Yet she did not feel hungry or thirsty. Or even sleepy. *Strange*, she thought.

At last Fernando came to a stop, and the rest did likewise.

"What is it? asked Tarak, looking around him wearily. "Why did you stop?"

"The Neptius is down there," said Fernando, pointing downwards.

Just then they realized they were on the edge of a gigantic crater. It must have been hundreds of feet deep.

"What are we waiting for then?" said Marissa. "Let's go and get the Neptius!"

"Yes, let's!" said Delta happily.

"Wait!" ordered Tarak. "This is not a trick, is it?" He glared suspiciously at the Wizard.

"No, of course not!" cried Fernando defensively. "Please, believe me!"

"Very well," said Tarak. "Go ahead!"

Fernando dived towards the center of the crater and they followed suit. It took them a minute or two before they reached the bottom. A strong, pungent smell at once assailed them. They quickly saw why. The entire crater was covered with flowers—All identical. About the size and shape of a tulip, they were a bright purple and speckled with dots of different colors.

"Strange flowers," commented Marissa, wrinkling her nose. "What are they?"

"They are Neptiuses," said Fernando.

"All of them?" frowned Marissa.

"Yes," was the simple reply.

"Is this a kind of joke?" demanded Tarak.

"No, not at all," replied Fernando.

"But there are millions of them!" cried Marissa. "How are we supposed to find *the* Neptius?"

"You mean the one I put a spell on? Well, if I remember correctly, I think I slightly clipped its petals. It will be quite recognizable. It's just a matter of finding it."

"It will take ages to do that!" gasped Delta.

"And we don't have the time," added Tarak. "This is hopeless."

"We'll just have to try," suggested Marissa.

"We might as well," agreed Elga. "What have we to lose?"

"What have we to lose?" mimicked Tarak. "The queen's life, that's what!.."

"Please, don't start that again!" pleaded Marissa. "You talk about wasting time and that's what we're doing now. Come on, let's get on with it!"

However, they didn't have the chance to begin their search. For just then the ground started shaking violently, just as it had done the first time Shantaya appeared. That seemed to be her calling card, everyone guessed.

"That's just great!" sighed Marissa.

"What do we do now?" whined Delta.

There wasn't time to do anything. And at that moment Shantaya materialized out of nowhere. Her sleigh swooshed to a stop.

"We meet again!" she crowed. "Well, it wasn't hard to guess where to find you!"

CHAPTER ELEVEN

"So, it's the Neptius you want?" cackled Shantaya, addressing Marissa more than anyone else. "Mmm, it's going to be a problem finding it." She tutted and shook her head. "So many neptiuses."

"If we can't find it, neither will you!" challenged Fernando, rather timidly.

"Be quiet you despicable creature!" snapped Shantaya. "You disgust me. I could've been queen of the undersea world by now and you my best general! But no, you were too weak with your stupid morals and sentiments!"

"At least I have feelings," mumbled Fernando.

"Feelings? sneered Shantaya. "Who needs them? Power is everything! Power rules! With it I can achieve anything I want!"

"Why haven't you then?" mocked Marissa.

"It's just a matter of time, don't you worry," retorted Shantaya.

"Humph!" went Marissa with a twinkle in her eyes. "You talk about power? I don't see it. I bet you don't even know where the Neptius is! Do you?"

"We shall see about that!" Shantaya seemed to take the challenge—and the bait. "Just you watch me!"

And she at once began to chant:

> *Neptius, oh, Neptius,*
> *Hear me, my precious,*
> *Wherever you are,*
> *Near or far,*
> *I don't care how,*
> *Show yourself now!*

The Nymph repeated these words over and over again and it appeared that the spell wasn't going to work. However, Shantaya persisted with her incantation, her voice rising higher and higher. Then somewhere in the middle of the crater a tiny orange light appeared at ground level. It began to glow brighter and brighter, then flicker on and off, flashing faster and faster, as if to indicate its whereabouts.

"Ah-ha!" cried Shantaya triumphantly. "Got you, my precious!"

"Quickly, Delta!" urged Marissa. "Let's get to the Neptius first! Go! Go now!"

Delta didn't need a second command as he darted

through the water like a torpedo! But to no avail. Shantaya had forestalled them, and in a flash, she reached the Neptius first.

"You see what power can do!" she boasted. "You can't do that with feelings! Can you, silly wizard?"

Poor Fernando looked utterly defeated. The same could be said about the rest. There was a long silence, apart from the rasping breath of the mollasks, whose eyes glowed triumphantly.

"What about you, land maid?" sniggered Shantaya. "Have you any powers?" And when Marissa remained silent, the Nymph went on, "I tell you what, I'll be nice and let you pick the Neptius. That's what you're here for, aren't you?"

She moved the sledge out of the way so that the flashing Neptius could be seen by everyone. True to what Fernando had said, the flower had two or three petals clipped.

"Go ahead," invited the nymph, smirking, enjoying the moment. "Help yourself, land maid, and you shall save the Queen!"

Marissa hesitated—she did not trust Shantaya. *Was she up to something?* she wondered. Of course, she was. But what? Even so, Marissa had to try, just out of curiosity, if nothing else.

Slipping off Delta's back, Marissa approached the Neptius tentatively. With a trembling hand, she reached for the flower, ever so slowly. Shantaya watched her all the time, still smirking, savoring the moment even more so.

Marissa braced herself as her fingers touched the Neptius. Her face twisted in a grimace, and with her heart thumping loudly in her chest, she suddenly plucked the Neptius—almost off its root! To her surprise nothing happened. She almost laughed with relief.

"Hurray!" cheered Delta, flapping his tail with delight.

"You've done it!" congratulated Elga.

"Thank you so much!" beamed Tarak who never looked so happy. "You have saved the Queen's life!"

"On the contrary!" corrected Shantaya, gloatingly. "You have just *killed* her!"

"What are you talking about?" frowned Marissa, still holding the Neptius which had now stopped flashing. "I've picked the Neptius and I'm a land mortal. The spell is now broken!"

"That's right," confirmed Fernando. "I know so."

"You are *so* naïve," Shantaya told him. "Do you think I didn't know where the Neptius was? Of course I did! Not only that, I knew the type of spell you cast on it. After all *I* taught you magic. Do you forget? All I had to do was to reverse the spell, so that if the Neptius is picked by a land mortal the Queen would die instantly! If you don't believe me, go back to the Palace and see for yourselves."

"You mean you're letting us go free?" asked Marissa, a little surprised.

"Why not?" shrugged Shantaya. "You are no use to me now. I have other important matters to deal with. I have an army to organize to assault the Palace. I shall be victorious. In a matter of days, I shall be crowned the new queen of the undersea world!" And saying no more, she departed.

"We must return to the palace immediately," said Tarak.

"It's the only way to find out," agreed Delta.

"We might as well," added Marissa.

"No," broke in Periwinkle. "We're not going back to the Palace."

"Why ever not?" asked Marissa. "We have to know for certain if Shantaya was telling the truth or not."

"The Queen is not in the Palace," said Periwinkle. "As a precaution she was moved to the Ancient Temple soon after she had fallen into a coma…"

"Why was I not informed about this?" demanded Tarak, angry and hurt at the same time. But he did not pursue the matter further. Perhaps he saw the sense in that.

"Yes, but even in the Ancient Temple is the Queen safer there?" Marissa wanted to know.

Periwinkle did not reply. Instead, he said to Tarak, "Please, lead us to the Ancient Temple. We must hurry!"

Still brooding Tarak complied.

"What about the Neptius?" said Marissa. "What do we do with it?"

"Get rid of it," Periwinkle told her. "It's of no use now."

"After all the trouble we've been through," said Marissa, shaking her head. "Goodbye, Neptius!" And she let the flower go.

Somewhat disappointed, Marissa turned to Fernando. "I don't understand," she said. "What is the Neptius to do with the spell, or vice-versa? I mean how did you cast the spell in the first place?"

"It was quite simple," replied Fernando sadly as though not wishing to be reminded of his wicked act. "When I cast the spell, I swore that the Queen would remain in a deep coma until the Neptius was picked by a land mortal. Of course, I meant myself. I never thought it possible for another land mortal to be here. But..." He paused to look at Marissa's hand in which she held Periwinkle. "I had not counted on the Drunes..."

"The Drunes?" interrupted Marissa. "What are they?"

"Well, er..." The wizard hesitated. "You know," he said, pointing to Periwinkle.

Marissa frowned, not understanding.

"Go ahead, tell her," said Periwinkle. "She needs to know."

This time Fernando did not look surprised when the seashell spoke as he had done so before when he was concussed.

"Well, er," began Fernando, still looking uncomfortable. "The Drunes are strange creatures with strange powers. They're as old as the sea itself. No one knows for certain where they originally came from. It is believed that they came from another world altogether—the only survivors of their kind. Being a marine species, they settled in the sea. However, it took them a long time to adapt and sadly most of them died. Possibly because the water in the sea is different from what they were used to. Perhaps because it's too salty for them, or too dense, or maybe it doesn't contain enough oxygen to suit their needs. There could be other reasons, of course. I don't really know. Finally, there remained only seven Drunes, and they are still the same number as far as I know. I'm pleased to say that they are doing very well."

"Thank you, Fernando," said Periwinkle. "You seem to know more than I do!"

The wizard didn't reply to that as he went on, "Although reserved creatures by nature, the Drunes are always willing to help and give advice when sought. As I said, they have great powers. But unlike Shantaya they use them only for a good purpose. They have helped the sea dwellers several times in the past and they continue to do so. It was they who made it possible for you to be here."

"What do you mean?" asked Marissa, a bit confused. It then suddenly dawned on her. "Oh, I see," she smiled. "Periwinkle is one of them—A Drune? Really?"

Fernando didn't answer that.

"Yes, yes, I am a Drune," said Periwinkle almost peevishly. "Now you know. And, yes, a Drune can acquire almost any desired shape," he went on to explain. "But only for a limited period of time, depending on the form acquired by the Drune. I was *chosen* for this particular task. Well, here I am—a mere seashell. I feel almost embarrassed!"

"Don't be!" laughed Marissa. "I just *love* seashells!"

To change the subject, Fernando asked, "Chosen, do you think Shantaya told us the truth? I mean about reversing the spell?"

"I fear she may have," Periwinkle replied.

"Then the Queen is…" Marissa couldn't bear to say the word.

But everyone knew what she was going to say. They waited for a reply in silence.

"It all depends," replied Periwinkle at length.

"On what?" asked Marissa.

"Well, it depends on when Shantaya changed the spell. If it's not long ago, the spell can be *re-reversed* if you see what I mean. If that's the case, the Queen's life may be saved."

"How can that be achieved?" enquired Tarak.

"I'm not sure," replied Periwinkle. "Not easily, that's for certain. But we must reach the Ancient Temple as soon as possible," he urged. "Time is important!"

CHAPTER TWELVE

At long last they were out of the nymph's territory, leaving behind the gloomy barren country of dull rocks and morbid vegetation. The water became brighter and lost its foul smell. Now Marissa was able to breathe clean, fresh air—a funny thing since she was underwater.

For some time, they travelled across a vast expanse of golden sand, which extended as far as the eye could see.

Presently they spotted in the distance something that looked like a giant egg. It stood up on one end, almost precariously, and glinted a deep silvery color.

Marissa was going to ask what it was, but Fernando forestalled her.

"That's the Ancient Temple. We'll be there shortly."

"Why is it called the Ancient Temple?" queried Marissa, curious.

"As the name implies," replied Fernando, "it's so old that no one knows how it came about. Even the Drunes are not quite sure. Isn't that correct, Chosen?"

"Yes, that's right," acknowledged Periwinkle. "We have tried to find out, but unsuccessfully. There's nothing mentioned in the ancient scrolls, some of which date from old times. Perhaps one day we will find out, but at the moment that remains a mystery."

"I see," said Marissa thoughtfully, although she didn't.

If the Drunes had come from another world, she mused, surely they must have travelled in some sort of craft. A spaceship perhaps? How else would it be possible for them to be here? It sounded quite logical to her.

As they approached the Ancient Temple, Marissa was convinced it was a spaceship. It was indeed shaped like a giant egg with the narrow end pointing upwards. It was huge, at least a hundred meters high, and its width half as long. It had porthole like windows along both sides, tinted a deep purple, but no visible doors. There must have been a least a dozen pods around it and some sort of rocket boosters, Marissa guessed. But whether still functionable or not no one could tell.

"Well," she said, "I'm not a rocket scientist, but that looks to me like a spaceship."

"A spaceship?" frowned Fernando, not understanding.

"Yes. It certainly looks like one."

"You mean a ship that flies? Like this…" With that Fernando made a gesture with his hands to imitate a bird in flight.

"Yes, if you like," said Marissa, amused.

Fernando burst out laughing. "I've never heard of such a ship! I know only of ships that sail across the seas."

"Pah," went Tarak, dismissively. "You're talking nonsense, land maid!"

Marissa was about to retort, *How would you know? You're a fish who never left the water!* But she restrained herself. She was fed up with clashing with the cantankerous senior royal guard. Besides she didn't think this was the time for arguments.

As though reading her mind, Periwinkle said, "I think we had better go and see how the Queen is doing. Please all of you remain here. Hopefully we will bring you good news."

Marissa slipped off Delta's back and swam towards the Ancient Temple.

"How do we get in?" she asked. She still couldn't see a visible entrance.

"Quite simple," said Periwinkle. "You see the red circle in front of you?"

Marissa couldn't miss it. "Yes, I do," she said.

"Place your hand close to it. The one in which you're holding me."

Marissa complied and waited. She knew she had to remain quiet. A short moment later, she felt her hand vibrate slightly. She could also hear a faint humming noise. This was how Periwinkle had summoned Delta on the beach, she remembered. It seemed ages ago now.

After a minute or so, a circular door slid open without a sound. Marissa couldn't tell whether it was operated electronically or by some other means. Magic perhaps?

"Go in, go in," prompted Periwinkle as Marissa hesitated.

Somewhat apprehensive she swam through the entrance as the door silently shut behind her. After they had gone through a long corridor, they came to a vast circular room. It was quite bare for its vastness. All Marissa could see was a round table with throne-like seats around it. She counted them in her head: *seven*. The same number as the Drunes. *Why does the number 'seven' seem to appear in a lot of stories*, thought Marissa—in myths, legends, fairy tales... She couldn't help smiling as she thought of "Snow White and the Seven Dwarfs".

"Keep going straight ahead of you," said Periwinkle. "Through that archway. There, can you see it?"

Marissa had to look carefully before she saw what Periwinkle meant. She had taken it to be just an alcove because it was only about six feet high and about four feet wide. It looked like a dark recess, well disguised to anyone who didn't know it was there.

"Huh, a secret entrance, is it?" said Marissa, but more to herself because Periwinkle did not reply to that.

Instead, he kept instructing her which way to go. They had gone through a maze of corridors, right and left, up and down, round and round, before they finally came to what looked like a dead end.

"We can't go any further," said Marissa, waiting for more instructions.

"Of course, we can," said Periwinkle.

Just then Marissa noticed a red circle on the blank wall.

"Oh, I see," she smiled. "Here we go again!" She was about to raise her hand close to the red circle when...

"Wait!" Periwinkle stopped her. "Please, listen. This is very important. I want you to promise me never to tell anyone what you're about to see. Keep it a secret to yourself. You see, no one has ever been in this room apart from the Drunes," he explained. "The only exception is of course the queen herself. And she was unconscious. We, the Drunes, brought her here. I hope you understand," finished Periwinkle.

"Of course, I do," said Marissa solemnly. "I promise I shall never tell anyone. Not even my cat, Tabitha!"

"That's very reassuring," said Periwinkle who hadn't a clue what Marissa was referring to. "Well, go ahead then."

Marissa did so. *Open sesame!* she felt like saying.

***

The first thing Marissa noticed as she entered the room was that the water here was warmer than anywhere else—that is in the undersea world. It was lighter too, and so much so that Marissa almost walked on the floor of the room rather than swim. Also, she noticed she could breathe much easier—More oxygen in the water perhaps? The room was square-shaped instead of being circular like all the rooms she had come across so far. And it was dim, almost dark.

"Go further up," instructed Periwinkle in a hushed voice.

Marissa complied, but hesitantly. For the first time, she noticed a dais-like platform at the bottom of the room. She had to squint hard to be able to distinguish it. Set on top were what looked like glass boxes, one beside the other and about a foot apart. They were oblong-shaped but with rounded ends and tops. They were tinged a dark green, but transparent enough. Again, Marissa counted them: *seven*. No surprise there! But what was in them? she wondered, curious and apprehensive at the same time.

As she approached the dais, she saw all seven boxes were occupied. In the one on the left was a mermaid. She lay on her back with her arms along her sides. She must be the queen, guessed Marissa.

The other boxes were occupied by purple, quaint-looking creatures. Marissa found them neither ugly nor beautiful—just somewhat strange. *These must be the Drunes, of course. But why are they all in boxes?* wondered Marissa. But she didn't ask that just yet. Instead, she stepped on the dais for a closer look.

Squatting by the Queen's box Marissa saw how astonishingly beautiful she was. She could tell even through the tinged glass. Her hair was the color of burning copper, cascading down in waves well below her waist. Her skin was a rosy pink and Marissa could guess how soft and delicate it must be. Her small, straight nose looked as if it had been meticulously carved by an artist, as well as her cupid-bow lips, which were strawberry-colored. Of course, she couldn't tell about the eyes, but Marissa imagined them to be to the color of a summer sky.

Bending even closer, Marissa saw the Queen's chest rising and falling slowly but rhythmically. She was breathing!

"The Queen is alive!" she whispered excitedly. "Oh, Periwinkle, I'm ever so glad!" She could hardly contain her delight, almost shouting with joy, and she was trembling all over.

"Yes, and most important she is merely sleeping and no longer in a coma," said Periwinkle, sounding relieved. "The Queen was brought here just in time. Otherwise…" His voice tailed off.

"You mean the Queen would've died had she remained in the Palace?"

"Yes," was the reply.

"But why?" Marissa wanted to know.

"Well, to put it simply," explained Periwinkle, "the box in which the Queen is resting is virtually time-less. One could remain there for a hundred years and yet would not age one single day. Yet, when you picked the Neptius, you were able to free her from the depths of the coma."

"That's amazing!" gasped Marissa. "How is that possible?"

"I'm afraid I don't know exactly why or how," replied Periwinkle. "We, the Drunes, found out about this a long time ago. Almost accidently you could say. We are still searching for answers regarding ourselves and our origin. We don't seem to know a lot. Perhaps the Ancient Temple holds the secrets and answers. Well, maybe one day, one day we'll... Oh, never mind that.

"To answer your first question, if Shantaya altered the spell before the Queen had been put in the time-less box, she would have certainly died by now. Of course, that cannot have been the case because the queen is free from the coma and quite alive. She's simply resting now and gaining her strength. You see, the spell was changed when the Queen was already safely protected in the time-less box. It acts as some sort of shield, but the Neptuis was still needed to set her free from the first incantation of the spell. The second incantation is now useless because the Queen is no longer in a coma—she has been freed."

"Yes, I think I understand now," nodded Marissa. "No, actually I don't," she quickly corrected herself. "I'm all muddled up, but I don't care. The Queen is safe and well and that's what really matters!"

"That is quite true," Periwinkle said in agreement. "However, Shantaya must not know about this. Not yet anyway. Once the Queen is fully awake, with the restorative powers from the time-less box, there is little Shantaya can do."

"Then the time-less box is more than just a shield? Can actually make the Queen stronger and even…" Marissa started to ask before being cut short by Periwinkle.

"I've said too much. Now, you must trust me and keep everything you have seen and everything you know quiet," implored Periwinkle.

"Is there anything I can do?" offered Marissa.

"No, no. Your task is done. You shall be returning home shortly. Shantaya is our concern. We, the Drunes, shall deal with her. Rest assured—we shall do everything in our power to destroy her. Evil never triumphs over good!"

"Oh, I know that!" said Marissa. She had read plenty books where "evil" and "good" clashed with the latter always prevailing. Of course, that also applied in the real world, she knew that too.

So far Marissa had barely taken notice of the Drunes in the other boxes. Her main concern had been the Queen who was now relatively safe. Squatting by the box next to the Queen's she peered through the tinged glass. She saw that it contained a creature resembling a squid. It had a large, orange head and four black eyes the size of saucers. At the sides of its head protruded two antenna-like stalks, similar to those of a snail. *Do they act as ears or some sort of sensors*, wondered Marissa. She couldn't really tell. The rest of the creature's body consisted of six long tentacles, a deep purple color.

What strange creatures, thought Marissa. *Is that what Periwinkle really looks like?*

She had a quick look at the remaining boxes and saw all the other Drunes looked exactly the same.

"Are they also in time-less boxes?" she asked.

"Yes," replied Periwinkle. "In fact, we spend a lot of time in them. That's how and why we have lived for so long. Incidentally," he added, "my box is occupied by the Queen."

"I gathered that," Marissa said with a smile. "Which is very kind of you." She paused, then asked, "But how do you wake up?"

"We set ourselves a time. We seem to be equipped with body clocks. They take care of that. It's our nature, I guess. Of course, it's different for the Queen. Her box has to be opened manually so to speak." Periwinkle seemed somewhat reluctant to speak about it. "Well, I guess we'd better go see the others. They must be anxious for our return!"

CHAPTER THIRTEEN

The rest of the party were indeed waiting anxiously outside the Ancient Temple. They didn't seem to have noticed Marissa when she showed up. Tarak was pacing to and fro restlessly. Delta stood still and appeared to be half asleep. Probably too tired. Elga was stretched on the sandy seabed, humming a soft, melancholy tune. Not far away Fernando sat cross-legged with his head bowed, childishly doodling with a stick. Of Sept there was no sign.

"Hello there!" Marissa had to shout to get their attention. "We're back!"

Tarak immediately came to a standstill. Delta woke up with a start. Elga and Fernando quickly got up. They all rushed to meet Marissa. She could tell by the look on her faces how desperate for news they were.

"The Queen is safe and sound for the moment," she

informed them. "She's asleep but no longer in a coma!" She struggled to not tell them any more than that. She had a secret to keep.

The good news cheered them all up. Elga came closer and kissed Marissa on both cheeks. "Thank you so much," she said gratefully. "You saved our Queen!"

"Oh, it wasn't really all me, I only picked the Neptius and..." Marissa started to speak before feeling Periwinkle vibrate ever so slightly in her hand. She held her tongue, as promised and allowed the others to celebrate.

"We owe you a lot, you know," added Delta, giving Marissa a gentle butt on the shoulder and a lick on the face.

Fernando, the most relieved of them all, also thanked Marissa. He shook hands with her which she found a bit awkward because his hand was slightly webbed. Even Tarak, surprisingly, gave her a warm, paternal hug. "We are indeed very grateful for all you have done," he said solemnly. "You may be stubborn and rude at times, but I must say you are a very brave land maid!"

Marissa nodded appreciatively, overwhelmed by their thanks and gratitude.

"It's all right," she said, blushing a little. "I'm glad I've been able to help. And I have enjoyed my adventure!" she added cheerfully, but she wasn't sure if that was the right thing to say. A life had been at stake. Thankfully it all ended well. Or at least it would soon, Marissa hoped.

"What do we do now?" asked Delta, excitedly. "Go back to the Palace and celebrate?"

"The celebrations can wait," said Periwinkle. "At least until Shantaya is dealt with for once and all. She still may pose problems. As for returning to the Palace, we must do that swiftly. Time is running out for me."

"You don't mean..." began Tarak, surprised and alarmed.

"Yes, I'm afraid so," said Periwinkle, his voice slightly weakening. "I cannot sustain my current form for very long. I shall soon be changing to a Drune once more...."

"Look!" interrupted Elga suddenly. "It's Sept, he's back!"

"I was wondering where he disappeared to," said Marissa with a smile.

"I think he just got fed up waiting," explained Elga. "He doesn't really know what's going on."

"But what's that behind him?" Delta cried out. "Something is chasing him, and it's huge!

"Oh, it must be Arka," said Periwinkle. "For some reason, she doesn't really like anyone around the Ancient Temple. We named her 'The Guardian'.

"Who's Arka?" asked Marissa.

"A whale," answered Periwinkle. "Probably the largest one that has ever existed!"

Marissa could well believe that. Arka appeared to be twice the size of Sept, or even more.

"It's all right, Arka won't hurt him," Periwinkle reassured everyone. "She will just chase him away from here."

Arka and Sept disappeared out of sight, but not for

long. They soon reappeared, and this time they were swimming side by side. They obviously enjoying each other's company.

"It looks as they've made friends," laughed Elga.

"They suit each other!" said Marissa.

"The Ancient Temple is a lot safer now with these two!" added Delta.

To change the subject to a serious matter, Tarak said, "Chosen, can you make it to the Palace? I'm thinking of the land maid."

"Truthfully, I don't think I'll get that far in my current form." Periwinkle's voice was ragged, clearly struggling to breathe. "Tarak, return to the palace. Explain what's happening. Tell them to prepare for an assault. By now Shantaya must have gathered her army of renegades and mutants. They could be heading towards the Palace this very moment. Take everyone with you, including Delta. I shall try and reach the Ancient Temple before I change. I think Marissa will be safe in there, until something has been arranged for her to return to her world. Quickly please. Hurry!"

The goodbyes were quick and rushed. But very emotional. There were kisses and hugs and shaking of hands. Tears as well. Marissa was sad to see everyone leave so suddenly. She had grown fond of them all—including Tarak.

"Bye! Bye!" she kept calling as they dwindled into the distance. Soon they disappeared out of sight. Sept soon joined them, leaving only Arka wandering around.

It was just then that Marissa realized she was struggling to breathe. It was as if someone had suddenly thrown a thick blanket over head. Periwinkle also realized that. "I'm changing quicker than I'd expected," he told Marissa, his voice slightly distorted. "I doubt whether there will be enough time to put you in a time-less box. I'm afraid it's too late!" It was not like him to panic, but he sounded really concerned. Marissa didn't reply. She hardly understood what the Drune was trying to tell her. But she knew she was in serious trouble. Since her adventure had begun, she had never really felt that her life could be in such imminent danger...Until now!

***

Marissa must have lost consciousness for a short moment. When she came to, she heard Periwinkle urging her to do something. She couldn't grasp the words—her head was spinning, her vision blurred, and she was about to pass out again.

"In there. Go inside! Please, hurry!" pleaded Periwinkle.

"What do you mean?" Marissa wanted to ask, but she couldn't. She then suddenly realized what Periwinkle was trying to tell her...

Arka the whale was a mere couple of feet away from her with her enormous mouth open wide.

"Take a deep breath and go inside!" urged Periwinkle

once more. "You shall be safe. Arka will take you to the surface. There's no other choice!"

True enough, thought Marissa: she *must* do it as bidden!

"Let go of me first!" Periwinkle reminded her. "Don't worry," he quickly added. "You should have enough oxygen in your lungs—I've made sure of that!"

Marissa trusted him of course, and she let go of him... Almost at once, Periwinkle changed into his original shape—a Drune, just like the other six in the time-less boxes.

She swam inside Arka's cavernous mouth. It was pretty dark and she just hoped Arka wouldn't swallow her accidently. Then the ride began. It was quite smooth considering the size of Arka. All the same Marissa had to hang firmly on to the whale's rough tongue. Just in case.

***

It was hard for Marissa to tell how long she had been inside Arka's mouth. While in the undersea world, she had lost all notion of time. She couldn't tell whether it was a couple of hours or days. *Strange*, she thought.

Sometime later Marissa heard a muffled sound like a big splash. Arka must have reached the surface of the sea, she guessed. In any case, the whale had stopped moving.

Just then Arka's mouth opened and bright sunlight

flooded in, dazzling Marissa. Instinctively she shielded her eyes with her hands. Clean, fresh air welcomed her, and she took one deep breath after another.

"Hurray!" she shouted jubilantly. "I've made it! I've made it!"

And so saying she scrambled out of Arka's mouth, slipping and skidding in her haste to get out, and clumsily fell into the water.

"Thank you, Arka!" she squealed with delight. "Thank you so much! You are the nicest whale I've ever met!"

The whale noisily spurted water out of her blowhole as if to say, "It's all right!" She did that a couple of times more, then gently and noiselessly she vanished below the surface of the water.

"Goodbye!" said Marissa, almost inaudibly. "Goodbye!"

She then began to swim a short distance towards the beach. To her surprise, it looked deserted. In fact, it was still morning. She could tell by the position of the sun—unless of course it was a different day altogether. If that were the case, her aunt would be worried sick about her. How would she explain everything to her? Or to anybody for that matter? No one would believe her anyway. Perhaps her fantastic adventure would have to remain a secret for the rest of her life.

However, Marissa's adventure was not to end here. For at that moment as she happened to glance back, she caught sight of something that made her heart jump into her mouth. It was Shantaya, riding her sledge at a tremendous speed.

"Oh, no!" cried Marissa, horrified. And she swam faster than she had ever done before.

The beach was just twenty yards or so away, but that looked like a mile to Marissa. Now the water was too shallow for swimming, so she stood up and started running instead. She could hear Shantaya doing likewise. The nymph must have discarded her sledge.

Suddenly a slimy, rubbery hand gripped Marissa's ankle firmly, and she fell. Shantaya towered above her, looking even more hideous above water than under it.

"Ha! Do you think you can escape me that easily?" smirked the nymph. "I told you we would meet again. I always keep my promise!"

"Keep away from me you ugly witch!" screamed Marissa, scuttling backwards. "I shall have you arrested! *Helppp!*" she shouted. But there was no one about to hear her. "What do you want with me?"

"I told you before, remember?" Shantaya pointed to Marissa's legs. "They're dreadful! You'd be much better off with a mermaid's tail. That's an experiment I've been looking forward to!"

"You're absolutely mad!" yelled Marissa angrily. "You're a butcher, experimenting on poor creatures against their will—turning them into hideous monsters!"

"I wouldn't call them that," sneered Shantaya. "I

think they're beautiful—a work of art! Now enough of this talk, you're coming with me. Like it or not!"

"I… I'm warning you," stuttered Marissa. "Kidnapping is against the law in my world… You'll go to jail for life! So, keep away from me!"

"Pah!" scoffed Shantaya dismissively. "Who cares about your stupid laws? It's *my* law that counts and I do what I want!" She sounded almost like a petulant child. "Now, do you come the easy way or the hard way? It doesn't really matter."

She suddenly stopped.

"What's happening to me?" she mumbled to herself. "What is it? I feel all weird. Is it you doing this?" she asked.

"Doing what?" Marissa cried, looking puzzled. "I'm not doing anything, so don't accuse me!"

She then noticed that Shantaya's spiky and ridiculous hair had begun to smoke. It sizzled and frizzled like sausages being fried. The air filled with an acrid smell.

"*Argghhh!*" shrieked the nymph. "My hair! What's happening to it? *Argghhh!*"

Desperately she tried to douse it with sea water, but that didn't seem to help. It burst into flames. Shantaya shrieked louder and longer, so much so that Marissa had to cover her ears with her hands. "Gosh, what's happening with her?" she thought, looking horrified.

Within seconds, all of the nymph's hair had burnt out.

"My lovely hair," she wailed pitifully. "All gone! My lovely hair!"

Marissa almost felt sorry for her, wicked as she was.

"You can always wear a wig," she tried to console. "You can have it any color or style you want!"

Shantaya glared at her, with murder in her eyes.

"You did it, didn't you?" she accused once more. "You did it! You're going to pay for it dearly! I shall turn you into the most hideous creature that ever existed!"

"Here we go again!" yelled Marissa, backing away. But she was terrified. She certainly did not feel sorry for the nymph now— not if she was going to turn her into a mutant or something worse.

However, she didn't have to worry about that, for just then just something else began to happen to the nymph. Something more gruesome. First her hands started to smoke. That soon extended to her arms—after that her legs. In a matter of seconds, the nymph's entire body was smoking. The stench was foul, sickening, and it made Marissa gag. Right before her eyes, Shantaya was melting as if she were made of wax.

"Yuck!" Marissa's stomach churned. "What's going on with her now?"

Before long, all that remained of the nymph was a large blob of horrid green stuff. It bobbed up and down with the water current. Not a pretty sight at all!

Marissa quickly moved away from it—just in case.

"What could've done that?" she grimaced, bewildered. "Maybe she's like a vampire. They don't like the sunlight either." She couldn't think of any other explanation.

"Out of your comfort zone I guess," she told the green disgusting blob which was now receding with the tide. "Goodbye!"

"Are you all right, love?" called a voice behind her. It was an old man on the beach, walking his dog.

"Yes, I'm OK," Marissa called back. "The nymph is dead, so everything is all right now. The Queen is safe!"

The man looked puzzled for a moment. He then said, "You should wear a hat. It's only morning but the sun is pretty hot."

"Yes," agreed Marissa. "You're quite right!"

The man smiled, he then called his dog, "Come along, Periwinkle!"

"Oh, my!" Marissa took a deep breath and ran all the way to her aunt's bungalow.

UNDERSEA EPILOGUE

Tarak, Delta and Elga reached the Palace without any mishaps and just in time to raise the alarm. The Senior Officer immediately deployed five hundred Royal Guards, who were ready to fight to the last one.

Shantaya's army had been expecting to storm the Palace by surprise and were themselves surprised, and they had to retreat. Soon however they attacked again, this time in a greater number.

From the outset, the battle was fierce and, sadly, lives were lost on both sides. The royal guards were outnumbered five to one, but they fought bravely.

Just when the nymph's army thought they were winning the battle, Sept and Arka fell upon them. This sudden and unexpected attack brought confusion among the enemy.

Shortly after, Fernando and about a hundred various creatures who had been captives of the nymph joined in the battle. Of course, the Wizard had freed them—his powers had evidently been restored.

The enemy was now in complete disarray; especially now that Shantaya was not there to organize them. For some reason, she had mysteriously disappeared. No one ever heard from her again.

The battle, however, raged on, fiercer and bloodier, the enemy retreating further and further away from the palace.

At long last, the nymph's army was completely routed. Some beat a hasty retreat, never to be seen again. Others were rightfully made prisoners, among them were the notorious One-Eyed and his gang.

A few days after this epic battle, the Queen was brought back to the Palace. She had recovered completely. Periwinkle, the Chosen, had the privilege to inform her about the latest events. And how she praised Marissa for her bravery. She wished she had met the land maid to thank her personally for saving her life and helping to bring peace to the undersea world.

Fernando sought forgiveness from the Queen, and she granted it to him. Not only that, she offered him to become her personal advisor. Of course, he humbly and gratefully accepted. Elga, young as she was, became the Queen's First Lady in Waiting. Delta was honored to be made the Royal Messenger. His job involved carrying important messages from one part of the kingdom to another. Periwinkle, the Drune, after his exhausting task, returned to the Ancient Temple to rest in his time-less box. Sept and Arka became very best friends. Sometimes they acted as bodyguards to the Queen. Not that she needed any because peace had returned to the undersea world.

Unbeknown to Marissa, she had become a legendary heroine in the undersea world. In her honor, a full-size statue was erected in the main courtyard of the Palace. It stood proud and majestic, admired by young and old alike, and much talked about. It stands there to this day.

As for Marissa, every year she spent her summer holidays with her aunt as she normally did. Tempted as she was, she never told anyone about her fantastic adventure in the undersea world. Not even her cat, Tabitha.

Now whenever Marissa came across a quaint and beautiful seashell, she would smile and simply walk on. "Let someone else pick it up. I've had my adventure thank you very much!"

About the Author

A H Benjamin is an international children's author who has been writing books since the mid-eighties. He has been published by Andersen Press, O.U.P, Little Tiger Press, Franklin Watts, Q.E.D and Tiger Tales (Penguin Random House). He has written over 50 books which have sold worldwide with more than 25 translations including Chinese, Korean, Turkish, Afrikaans, Greek and Arabic. His books are very popular in schools, book clubs and especially libraries, ranking among the highest in the UK Public Landing Right. In addition, some of his work have been adapted for radio, television and theatre. AH Benjamin will have two new picture books published through Notable Kids in 2023 and 2024. He lives in Lincolnshire with his wife, Trisha. They have four grown up children and six young grandchildren who have all been an inspiration to him.